KHUSHWANT SINGH ON HUMOUR

Born in Punjab's Hadali village (now in Pakistan) in 1915, Khushwant Singh was among India's best-known and most widely read authors and journalists. He was founder–editor of *Yojana*, and editor of *The Illustrated Weekly of India*, *National Herald* and *Hindustan Times*. His first book, *The Mark of Vishnu and Other Stories*, was published in 1950. He published six novels—*Train to Pakistan*, *I Shall Not Hear the Nightingale* (retitled *The Lost Victory*), *Delhi: A Novel*, *The Company of Women*, *Burial at Sea* and *The Sunset Club*. Among his other books are an autobiography, *Truth, Love and a Little Malice*, and a two-volume history of the Sikhs. In addition, he published translations of Hindi and Urdu novels.

Khushwant Singh was a member of the Rajya Sabha from 1980 to 1986. He was awarded the Padma Bhushan in 1974, which he returned in 1984 to protest the siege of the Golden Temple by the Indian Army. In 2007, he was awarded India's second highest civilian honour, the Padma Vibhushan.

Khushwant Singh died in 2014.

KHUSHWANT SINGH ON HUMOUR

Selected Writings

Edited by MALA DAYAL

Published by
Rupa Publications India Pvt. Ltd 2018
161-B/4, Gulmohar House,
Yusuf Sarai Community Centre,
New Delhi 110049

Sales centres:
Bengaluru Chennai
Hyderabad Kolkata Mumbai

Copyright © Mala Dayal 2018
Anthology copyright © Mala Dayal 2018
The Acknowledgements (on page 133–134) are an extension of
the copyright page.

The views and opinions expressed in this book are the author's own and the facts are as reported by him which have been verified to the extent possible, and the publishers are not in any way liable for the same.

While every effort has been made by the editor to trace copyright holders and obtain permission, this has not been possible in all cases; any omissions brought to our attention will be remedied in future editions.

All rights reserved.

No part of this publication may be reproduced, transmitted, or stored in a retrieval system, in any form or by any means, electronic, mechanical, photocopying, recording or otherwise, without the prior permission of the publisher.

P-ISBN: 978-93-5304-015-4
E-ISBN: 978-93-5304-016-1

Seventh impression 2025

10 9 8 7

Printed in India

This book is sold subject to the condition that it shall not, by way of trade or otherwise, be lent, resold, hired out, or otherwise circulated, without the publisher's prior consent, in any form of binding or cover other than that in which it is published.

For Pami,
whose sense of humour has often got him in trouble

Contents

Editor's Note ix

1. Humour—an Antibiotic against Hate 1
2. Political Humour 17
3. Community Jokes 36
4. Sardarji Jokes 40
5. Ha Ha Honoris Causa 50
6. The Joys of Farting, and the Pleasure of Pissing 58
7. Nose-picking 65
8. Name-dropping 68
9. How to Appear Learned Without Learning 71
10. Talking Shop 74
11. Nick to the Name 76

12. English-Vinglish	81
13. Irony, Satire and Witty Terminology	93
14. Outraged Correspondence	101
15. Torture by Telephone	103
16. Pakistani Humour	106
17. Cricketing Humour	117
18. Being Tipsy	119
19. Black Humour	122
Acknowledgements	133

Editor's Note

My father's favourite bedtime reading was joke books. He had a fairly large collection which he dipped into every night. He also enjoyed the company of those (specially beautiful women) who were witty and could tell jokes well. His own joke books were well-known and sold better than his novels or non-fiction. But, over the years, besides the joke books he had compiled, he had written several humorous pieces—some long, some very short. A selection of these have been compiled in this book. I hope they will, if not raise a laugh, bring a smile.

I

Humour—an Antibiotic against Hate

Do we Indians have a sense of humour? I would answer the question in one word. No. Sense of fun, yes. Laughter, yes. Wit, sometimes. Sarcasm and irony, often. Sense of humour, never. What passes for the Indian sense of humour is no laughing matter. It may occasion a smile. More often it makes you want to squirm.

You may well ask, how can you differentiate between laughter, wit, sarcasm, irony on the one hand and a sense of humour on the other? I reply, 'Don't ask me for definitions because the best I can do is to quote different dictionaries. And that will not get us anywhere.' James Thurber, America's best-known humorist of recent years, defined humour as 'a kind of emotional chaos told calmly and quietly in retrospect'. Quite frankly, I don't understand what Thurber was talking about. I much prefer the description of a humorist as 'a comedian who doesn't tell dirty stories'. Even this is not really satisfactory as I am often regarded as an Indian humorist though I am no comedian and I tell a lot of dirty stories.

Humour is something very subtle and therefore eludes precise definition. I don't recall who said that it was like kicking someone so courteously that he is so delighted that he feels it was the other fellow who got his ass kicked. It makes you laugh at what would make you mad if it happened to you. The closest anyone can get to labelling a humorist was Hunt who described him as 'one who shows faults of human nature in such a way that we recognize our failings and smile—and our neighbours' failings and laugh'. Humour is not hurtful. On the contrary, it is an antibiotic against hate. That's as close as I can get to defining a sense of humour.

Now let me analyse why we as a nation are lacking in it. The first condition, the sine qua non—without which nothing humorous can be created—is our inability to laugh at ourselves. We take ourselves too seriously and are easily offended by those who do not share our self-esteem. Sometime or the other, every one of us makes an ass of himself. But how rare it is to hear an Indian tell a joke about himself in which he is shown in a poor light!

This is especially true of politicians who have notoriously thin skins. We have had quite a few very good political cartoonists—Shankar Pillai, R.K. Laxman, O.V. Vijayan, Rajinder Puri, Mario Miranda. Their cartoons have enlivened our newspapers and magazines and brought a smile to our faces. But many politicians and political parties take themselves very seriously and consider far too many topics as sacred cows not to be laughed about. They take umbrage at being the butt of jokes. Laughter for them is no laughing matter. They serve those who poke fun at them with legal notices—or worse.

This is a true story about a minister of government. You know what most of our ministers are like! No sooner do they become powerful than they lose all sense of proportion and get inflated with self-esteem. Well, this minister I am going to tell you about was an exception to the general rule of arrogance and exaggerated importance. I saw him sitting all by himself in a corner of a restaurant. I went up to him and invited him to join my friends. He graciously agreed to do so. I introduced him and added, 'My friends were saying that of all the important people in this country, you are the only one who has not lost his head and retains his sense of modesty.'

The minister blushed to the roots of his grey beard and replied, '*Hanji*, everyone says I am very modest. In school and college, I never stood second in my class [in case you don't know, that is an Indianism for saying you always topped] but

I never gave up my modesty. I had the biggest legal practice in my district, but I never gave up my modesty. And now I am the youngest ever person to be made a full minister but I remain as modest as ever.'

With great difficulty I kept myself from breaking out into guffaws of laughter. But I couldn't retain this gem, illustrative of our national character, in my belly for too long. I narrated the dialogue at many parties and also wrote about it saying that as a nation we were unable to stomach success and even a modest Indian was not happy unless he could prove himself to be the most modest man in the world. Needless to say, all this got back to the minister. He never forgave me for making him out to be a bit of an ass. And once when I went to see him to ask for a favour he dismissed me very curtly, '*Aap mera mazaak uratey rahtey hain* (You keep making fun of me).'

Another anecdote, also true, is about a young and very bright student who had topped in every exam he took and ended up with a scholarship at Oxford University where also he got a first class first. He became a kind of guru and gave sermons on the Vedanta. The main theme of the message he preached was that the source of all evil was *hum hain* (I am), the ego which inflated into *ahamkara* (arrogance). And that unless you conquered this ego, you could not hope to better yourself. One day, one of his disciples asked him, 'Sir, I agree with all you say, but how exactly does one conquer one's ego?'

'A very good question,' replied our philosopher. 'I know something about the problem of conquering the ego. Because of my many achievements it is much tougher for me than for any of you. I recommend that each one of you devise your own formula. What I do is sit [in] padmasana and repeat to myself every morning and evening, "I am not so-and-so who stood first in every exam I took. I am not so-and-so who broke all examination records of my university. I am not so-and-so who became president of the university union. I am not so-and-so the most brilliant philosopher of the Orient. I am merely a spark of the divine."'

Needless to say that those of us who spread this story about the formula to conquer the ego came in for some very uncharitable lambaste from this human spark of the divine.

* * *

But we do have a tradition of humour coming down to us from ancient times. Our ancients poked fun at their kings, statesmen and army commanders. They were lampooned as important men controlled by their wives and mistresses who offloaded their bastard children on their unsuspecting husbands. Then we had court jesters like Birbal, Tenali Raman and Gopal Bhore. They specialized in solving riddles put to them by their patrons or scoring points against other royal advisers. Their sense of humour was not sophisticated but they continue to enjoy esteem among common people to this day. Every generation of Indians has produced its own humorists. I may be the one for the present generation.

I have a large collection of jokes: some I make myself, others I pick up from friends or books and remould to suit me. A large number were sent to me by readers who have been acknowledged by name. Several slim volumes of my jokes liberally contributed to by readers have been published and sell better than any of my other books. I get the royalties; my contributing readers only get the pleasure of seeing their names in print. The joke, as usual, is on them.

At the end of the day, more than my other works as a novelist, short story writer, historian of the Sikhs or translator, I am known for my joke books. At every gathering, I am implored, '*Koi joke-shoke ho jai* (Let there be a joke or two).' I am known as a joker. Unfortunately, most of my best jokes are unprintable because they have to do with sexual aberrations. What is a joke if it hasn't something to do with sex? Book censors don't see it that way.

Let me mention some jokes contributed by others:

Humour–an Antibiotic against Hate

A Hindu, a Muslim and a Sikh were discussing the marvellous achievements of their own brands of surgery. Said the Hindu, 'I know of a vaidji who joined a severed arm with the use of Ayurvedic glue. You can't even tell where the arm had been cut.' Not to be outdone, the Muslim spoke, 'A hakim sahib has evolved a new kind of adhesive ointment. He used it on a fellow who had his head cut off. You can't tell where the neck was severed.' It was the Sardarji's turn to extol the latest developments in Sikh surgery. 'We have gone much further,' said the Sardarji thumping his chest proudly. 'There was this chacha of mine who was cut into two around his navel. Our Sikh surgeon immediately slaughtered a goat and joined its rear half to chacha's upper half. So now we have our chacha as well as two litres of milk every day.'

Actor-wrestler Dara Singh, taking a stroll along Juhu beach, was set upon by a dozen urchins who, after beating him black and blue, took away his purse which, fortunately for him, contained very little money. Dara, who had floored the world's best wrestlers, put up no resistance. When he arrived home with two black eyes, puffed cheeks and a torn shirt, his Sardarni asked him in great alarm what had happened. Dara Singh told her all.

'And why didn't you hit back? Surely you could have knocked the hell out of these skinny fellows!'

'Sure!' replied the Sardar. 'But my fee for flooring champions is ₹25,000. I don't fight for free.'

Sukhwinder and Dukhwinder were close friends. They used to meet at a bar every evening, occupy the same table, sit opposite each other, and order two glasses of raw rum, drink them in one gulp and walk away. This continued for some years. One day while stepping out of the bar after the drinks, Sukhwinder collapsed. He was carried to the station sick quarters. Doctors attending on him declared him dead.

Dejected, Dukhwinder went alone to the bar next evening and ordered two glasses of rum. When the waiter placed the two glasses of rum on the table, Dukhwinder first sat on Sukhwinder's chair, drank the rum and then came to his chair and drank his glass.

Out of curiosity, the waiter asked him, 'Sir what is this?'

To that, Dukhwinder replied, 'Sukhwinder is no more, he expired yesterday, so I have to continue drinking his quota first and then mine; otherwise his soul will never rest in peace.'

This continued for a year.

One evening, he entered the bar and ordered only one glass.

He sat on Sukhwinder's chair, drank it and got up to leave the bar. The waiter again asked him, 'Sir, why only one glass today?'

To that, Dukhwinder replied, 'I am expecting a call from Bade Miyan (the Almighty) at any moment, so before that, I want to get rid of all my vices. Alcoholism being one of them, I have stopped drinking from today. Henceforth I will come to the bar every evening to drink for Sukhwinder only.'

☺

Telling a lie is a fault for a little boy, an art for a lover, an accomplishment for a bachelor and a matter of survival for a married man.

☺

A man dies and goes to hell. There, he finds that there is a different hell for each country. He goes to the German hell and asks, 'What do they do here?' He is told, 'First they put you in an electric chair for an hour. Then they put you on a bed of nails for another hour. Then the German devil comes in and beats you for the rest of the day.'

The man does not like the sound of that at all. So he moves on and checks the US hell, as well as the Russian hell, and the hell of many more countries. He discovers that they are all more or less the same as the German hell.

Then he comes to the Indian hell and finds that there is a long line of people waiting to get in. Amazed, he asks, 'What do they do here?' He is told, 'First they put you in an electric chair for an hour. Then they put you on a bed of nails for another hour. Then the Indian devil comes and beats you for the rest of the day.'

'But that is exactly the same as in all the other hells. So why are so many people waiting to get in here?' asks the man. 'Because the maintenance is so bad that the electric chair does not work. Someone has stolen all the nails from the bed, and the Indian devil is a former government servant. So he comes in and signs the register and then goes to the canteen!'

The young and pretty chambermaid at the five-star hotel asked the upstart client she had just shown to his room. 'What time would you like to be woken up, Sir?'

'At seven,' replied the over-smart guest, 'and with a kiss.'

'Very well, Sir,' said the girl, as she retreated down the corridor. 'I will leave your message with the night watchman.'

Humour–an Antibiotic against Hate

A Parsi of ill repute chose to seek forgiveness for his sinful ways through baptism. So he decided to recast his will. Instead of a Zoroastrian priest, he summoned his lawyer and his doctor, and asked them to stand on either side of his deathbed. 'Why do you want us beside you at this time?' they asked. Replied the recently baptised Zoroastrian, 'I want to die like Jesus Christ, with two thieves on either side of me.'

Love thy neighbour's neighbour. To err is human; to blame others is good politics. Self before service. Be Indian, buy foreign. An onion a day, keeps everybody away. Behind every unsuccessful man, there are many women.

I was once travelling from Rohtak to Gurgaon in the Roadways bus. The conductor was quite agitated and grumbling after having a tiff with a passenger over counting of the change. His loud declaration was: 'I don't bother about anybody, even if he is the owner of many factories. I don't bother about anybody, even if he is the owner of a fleet of cars. I don't even bother about the chief minister of the state.'

I could not but ask him, 'Dear friend, you seem to have

the gift of the gab. Can you tell me the source of your strength that you don't even bother about the chief minister?'

He replied very nonchalantly, 'The chief minister is no match for me. He distributes 90 tickets once in five years, whereas I distribute 500 tickets daily of my own accord. Now you can measure the difference.' I was floored and kept quiet throughout the journey.

In the US they invented a machine that catches thieves. They took it to different countries for a test. In the US itself, in 30 minutes the machine caught 20 thieves; in the UK, in 30 minutes it caught more than 50 thieves; in Spain, in 30 minutes it caught 65 thieves; in Ghana, in 30 minutes it caught 600 thieves. But in India, they caught nobody—in 15 minutes the machine was stolen. I told you not to laugh.

May I request you, 'a great communist', to change the already mutilated name, Kolkata, to Kolkatai. This minor change of 'i' after Kolkata will dramatize the journey from the Middle East to the Far East. Look at it this way. One leaves Dubai *and lands at Mumbai, and from there, at Chennai. And from Chennai to Kolkatai (if you kindly agree), and from there, to Shanghai. All the five airport names will end in 'ai' and give a boost to our failing AI (Air India).*

☺

A policeman's son fared badly in his half-yearly examinations. The father was very angry and was about to thrash him when the boy took out a fifty-rupee note from his pocket and said, 'Daddy, yeh lo aur mamley ko rafa-dafa kar do (Take it Daddy and let the matter end here).'

☺

A blonde walks into a bank in New York City and asks for the loan officer. She says she's going to Europe on business for two weeks and needs to borrow $5,000. The officer says the bank will need some kind of security for the loan, so the blonde hands over the keys to a new Rolls-Royce. The car is parked on the street in front of the bank, she has the title and everything checked out. The bank agrees to accept the car as collateral for the loan.

The bank's president and its officers all enjoy a good laugh over the blonde's using a $250,000 Rolls as collateral against a

$5,000 loan. An employee of the bank then proceeds to drive the Rolls into the bank's underground garage and parks it there.

Two weeks later, the blonde returns, repays the $5,000 and the interest, which comes to $15.41. The loan officer says, 'Miss, we are very happy to have had your business, and this transaction has worked out very nicely, but we are a little puzzled. While you were away, we checked you out and found out that you are a multimillionaire. What puzzles us is why would you bother to borrow $5,000?'

The blonde replies, 'Where else in New York City can I park my car for two weeks for only $15.41 and expect it to be there when I return?'

This guy was hitch-hiking on a real dark night in the middle of a thunderstorm. Time passed slowly and no cars went by. It was raining so hard he could hardly see his hand in front of his face. Suddenly, he saw a car slowly approaching and appearing ghostlike in the rain. It slowly crept towards him and stopped.

Wanting a ride real bad, the guy jumped in the car and closed the door. Only then did he realize that there was nobody behind the wheel. The car slowly started moving and the guy was terrified, too scared to think of jumping out and running. He saw that the car was slowly approaching a sharp curve.

He started to pray and beg for his life; he was sure the car would go off the road and into the bayou and he would surely drown, when just before the curve, a hand appeared through the driver's window and turned the steering wheel, guiding the car safely around the bend.

Paralyzed with fear, the guy watched the hand reappear every time they reached a curve. Finally, the guy, scared to near death, had all he could take and jumped out of the car, and ran to the town. Wet and in shock, he went to a bar and ordered two shots of whiskey, then told everybody about his supernatural experience.

About half an hour later, two guys walked into the bar and one said to the other, 'Look, there's the idiot that rode in our car when we were pushing it in the rain.'

Bill and Sam, two elderly friends, met in the park every day to feed the pigeons, watch the squirrels and discuss the world's problems. One day, Bill didn't show up. Sam didn't think much about it and figured that Bill might have had a cold or something. But after Bill hadn't shown up for a week or so, Sam really got worried. However, since the only time they ever got together was in the park, Sam didn't know where Bill lived, and so was unable to find out what had happened to him.

A month passed, and Sam figured he had seen the last of Bill. But one day, Sam approached the park and—lo and behold—there sat Bill! Sam was very excited and happy to see Bill and told him so.

Then he said, crying out loud, 'Bill, what in the world happened to you?'

Bill replied, 'I have been in jail.'

'Jail?' cried Sam. 'What in the world for?'

'Well,' Bill said, 'you know Mary, that cute little blonde waitress at the coffee shop where I sometimes go?'

'Yeah,' said Sam, 'I remember her. What about her?'

'Well, one day, she filed rape charges against me. At 89 years of age, I was so proud that when I got to the court, I pleaded guilty. The judge served me a sentence of 30 days for perjury.'

2

Political Humour

With so many taboos regarding who and what we can joke about, what are we left with? Precious little. Turn the pages of any of our magazines. Most of them devote a page or so to what they think is humorous. The most popular form is an item entitled 'Answers to Your Questions' where readers' queries are answered by a hired wit or by the editor himself. When I read them I do not know whether to laugh or cry. The other item usually bears some silly title like 'Smile Awhile', 'Laugh', 'Laffs' or 'Laughing Matter'.

Without exception, all the jokes printed under this heading are taken from some international syndicates or lifted from foreign magazines and occasionally rephrased to make them sound Indian. Almost all the strip-cartoons and comics are likewise taken from foreign sources. I have a sizeable collection of books on humour; I have yet to come across one on Indian humour which is not almost entirely plagiarized.

What we do have in plenty, however, are PJs (*phlat* jokes). I am tempted to compile an anthology of India's worst jokes. I suspect the largest section will be devoted to Sardarjis by non-Sardarjis. Sardarjis on themselves are usually more subtle and witty.

O.P. Goel, from Delhi University, sent me one which he says is currently very popular on the campus. It only confirms my opinion that Delhi has a higher proportion of morons than any other city of India.

A Punjabi (you may call him a Sardarji if that makes it sound funnier) walking along the beach saw a flock of birds fly overhead, calling to each other. In the belief that they wished to speak to him, he enquired, 'Birdie, Birdie kee gal hai (What are you doing or saying)?'

One of the birds paused in its flight and replied, 'Sardie, Sardie, seagull hai.'

The only comment I can make is the teenagers' response to a PJ. 'Tickle, tickle.'

Political Humour

A rich source of humour in all countries are state legislatures and parliaments. This particular brand of humour requires a ready wit so that the retort can be fired back as soon as a remark is made, not thought of much later: what the French call the staircase wit—something you think you should have said going down the stairs after the party is over. We have some parliamentarians who were quick-witted in their repartees but for the life of me I cannot recollect anything really memorable.

Let me narrate some that have stayed in my memory. One of my favourites is from the Haryana Assembly. A lady member of the opposition was fiercely attacking the chief minister and his government. The chief minister lost his temper and described the lady member as *charitraheen* (woman of loose character). The lady was understandably furious and roundly abused the chief minister describing his mother, wife, sisters and daughters as *charitraheen*. There was an uproar in the House. The Speaker had the exchange of abuse expunged from the record and ordered both of them to apologize to each other. The chief minister made amends and asked the lady to forgive him and added, 'I regard her as my own sister.' When it came to the lady's turn to apologize, she said, 'I concede your sister is not *charitraheen*. But I cannot say anything about your other family relatives who I don't know.'

Mrs Gandhi's late husband, Feroze Gandhi, was known for his sharp sense of repartee. But the one repartee most often quoted seems to have been thought out well ahead of the time of its delivery. The unhappy recipient of Feroze's barbed shaft was the then Finance Minister, T.T. Krishnamachari. Old TTK, as he was known to friends, had a very acid tongue and had been known to refer to Feroze Gandhi as the then Prime Minister Nehru's lapdog. Feroze's opportunity came when he had to open the debate on the Mundhra scandal in which TTK's name was involved. As he came into the House, he went up to the treasury benches and addressed the finance minister, 'TTK, I believe you have been describing me as a lapdog. You no doubt regard yourself as a pillar of the state. Today, I will do to you what a lapdog does to a pillar.'

These make a very poor collection when you compare them to the sallies of wit and humour fired by A.P. Herbert, Aneuran Bevan and, above all, Winston Churchill in the British House of Commons. I will not narrate them as most of you are likely to have heard them before. But let me tell you an absolute gem of a retort that I picked up from, of all places, the Parliament of Uruguay. An opposition member was attacking a minister. The minister got up to intervene.

The member shouted back, 'But I haven't finished yet.' This was repeated many times but every time the minister rose to defend himself the opposition man yelled, 'Sit down! I haven't finished yet.' When at long last the man finished his speech, the minister asked, 'Have you finished now?'

'Yes,' replied the man taking his seat. 'Then pull the chain,' snapped the minister amidst thunderous applause.

Politicians have always been popular subjects for jokes, especially those who were dictatorial or authoritarian. This joke was told during the time Indira Gandhi imposed Emergency on the country.

Bapu Gandhi in heaven was very perturbed that after all he had done for the country no one really bothered about him anymore. So he sent for Nehru, who was also in heaven, and asked him, 'Nehru, what did you do all the years you were prime minister to perpetuate my memory?'

Nehru replied, 'Bapu, I did all I could. I had a samadhi made at the spot where we cremated you. Twice in the year, your birthday and the day of your assassination, we collected in the thousands to sing "Ram Dhun" and pay homage to you.'

Bapu was satisfied with Nehru's answer. He sent for Lal Bahadur Shastri and put to him the same question. 'Bapu, I had a very short time as prime minister,' replied Shastri. 'In those two and a half years I had all your works and speeches translated into all the Indian languages and put in village libraries.'

Gandhi was satisfied. 'Who became PM after you?' he asked.

'It is Nehru's chhokri (daughter) who is ruling the country now,' he replied.

So Bapu sent for Indira Gandhi and put the same question to her. Indira replied, 'I've done more to perpetuate your memory than either my father or Shastri. I've made the entire populace like you and left them with nothing more than a loincloth of the type you wear and a stick of the sort you carry.'

Bapu was very alarmed. 'You mustn't do this. The people will rise in rebellion against you,' he warned.

'I've taken care of that,' replied Indira. 'I have put the langotee around their necks and shoved the danda up their bottoms.'

Lalu Prasad Yadav has also often been a source of humour. One I remember was about his applying for a job in the USA.

Lalu Prasad sent his biodata to apply for a post in Microsoft Corporation USA. A few days later he got the reply.

Political Humour

Dear Mr Lalu Prasad,
You do not meet our requirement. Please do not send any further correspondence. No phone call shall be entertained.
Thanks,
Bill Gates

Lalu Prasad jumped with joy on receiving this reply. He arranged a press conference:

'Bhaiyon aur behno, aap ko jaan kar khushi hogee ki hum ko Amreeca mein naukri mill gayee hai (*Brothers and sisters, you will be happy to know that I have got a job in America*).' Everyone was delighted.

Lalu Prasad continued, 'Ab hum aap sab ko apna *appointment* letter padkar sunaaongaa. Par *letter* angreezee main hai isliyen saath-saath *Hindi* mein *translate* bhee karoonga (*Now I will read out my appointment letter to you. But because the letter is in English, I will also translate it in Hindi*).'

Dear Mr Lalu Prasad 'Pyare *Lalu Prasad* bhaiyya.' **You do not meet** 'aap to miltey hee naheen ho'... **our requirement** 'humko to zaroorat hai.' **Please do not send any further correspondence** 'ab letter vetter bhejne ka kaouno zaroorat nahee.' **No phone**

call 'phoonwa ka bhee zaroorat nahee hai,' ***shall be entertained*** 'bahut khaatir kee jayegi.'
Thanks 'aapka bahut bahut dhanyavad.'
Bill Gates 'Bilva.'

Then there are anti-establishment jokes such as the following:

An American delegation on a visit to India was being shown around the capital. In the evening they were taken to the secretariat for a panoramic view of Vijay Chowk and Rajpath. Came the closing hour and thousands of clerks poured out of their offices. The place was crammed with bicycles and pedestrians.

'Who are all these people?' asked the leader of the American delegation.

'They are the common people of India; the real rulers of the country,' proudly replied the minister accompanying the visitors.

A few minutes later came a fleet of flag-bearing limousines escorted by pilots on motorcycles followed by jeeps full of armed policemen. 'And who are these?' asked the American.

'These are us,' replied the minister with the same pride, 'the servants of the people.'

Political Humour

A vagrant, finding no place on the pavement, parked himself at the feet of the statue of Mahatma Gandhi. At midnight, he was awakened by someone gently tapping him with his stick. It was the Mahatma himself.

'You Indians have been unfair to me,' complained the benign spirit. 'You put my statues everywhere that show me standing or walking. My feet are very tired. Why can't I have a horse like the one Shivaji has? Surely, I did as much for the nation as he! And you still call me your Bapu.'

Next morning, the vagrant went around calling on several ministers. At long last he persuaded one to join him for a night-long vigil at the feet of the Mahatma's statue. Lo and behold, as the iron tongue of the neighbouring police station gong struck the midnight hour, the Mahatma emerged from his statue to converse with the vagrant. He repeated his complaint of having to stand or walk and his request to be provided a mount like the Chhatrapati's.

'Bapu,' replied the vagrant, 'I am too poor to buy you a horse, but I have brought this minister of government for you. He...'

Bapu looked at the minister and remarked, 'I asked for a horse, not a donkey.'

An argument arose as to which state government excelled in corruption. The following story settled the issue:

An MLA from Kerala visited Chandigarh and called on a Punjab minister at his house. He was amazed at the ostentation and asked his old friend, 'How did you manage to acquire so much wealth?'

'Are you really interested to know?'

'Of course. A little extra knowledge always helps.'

'Then wait till tomorrow, and I shall explain fully.'

The next day, the minister drove the MLA down the highway for several kilometres in his personal Honda. He stopped the car, both of them got out and the minister pointed his finger to a spot down the beautiful valley.

'Do you see the big bridge over there?' he asked.

'Yes,' replied the MLA.

'Half the cost of the bridge went into my pocket.'

Four years later, the Punjabi who in the meantime had lost his ministership, went on a holiday to Trivandrum and called on his old friend, who had now become a minister. 'By God,' said the Punjabi, 'you have beaten me flat. Crystal chandeliers, Italian marble, Mercedes. Tell me how you managed it.'

'I will tell you tomorrow,' said the minister.

Next day, the minister drove him down the highway, stopped the car at a spot overlooking a valley and the minister pointed his finger to a spot down the valley and asked, 'Do you see the bridge over there?'

'I see no bridge,' said the Punjabi.

'Quite right,' said the minister. 'The entire cost of the bridge went into my pocket.'

A minister of government whose knowledge of English was very poor was provided with a secretary to write speeches for him.

'Give me a 15-minute speech on the Non-aligned Movement,' ordered the boss.

The text was prepared to last exactly 15 minutes. But when the minister proceeded to make his oration it took him half an hour to do so. The organizers of the conference were upset because their schedule went awry. And the minister was upset because his secretary had let him down. He upbraided him. 'I asked for a 15-minute speech; you gave me a half-hour speech. Why?' he demanded.

'Sir, I gave you a 15-minute speech. But you read out its carbon copy as well.'

The Kashmir militants tried to kidnap one of Devi Lal's loved ones but gave up: They couldn't decide which buffalo to take hostage.

The greatest compliment our postal services paid me was the time when Bhindranwale was on the rampage in Punjab. It was from one of his admirers in Canada. The contents were in Gurmukhi and full of earthy abuses for me.

The address was in English: 'Bastard Khushwant Singh, India.'

Someone in our Postal Department put my correct address and the letter was delivered to me. My admiration for our postal services went up sky-high.

A lovely sample of bureaucratic wit of the days of the British Raj sent to me was an entry made by an executive engineer in the visitors' book of a circuit house:

'The veranda of the circuit house badly needs railings. During my momentary absence, a cow ate up some estimates which I had left lying on a table in the veranda.'

Below this note was the commissioner's observation:

'I find it hard to believe that even cows could swallow PWD estimates.'

Two tigers disappeared from the Delhi zoo. Not a trace could be found of them anywhere. Then suddenly, one day, six months later, they were back in their cages. One was skin and bones; the other had put on a lot of weight. They began to compare notes. Said the thin tiger, 'I was very unlucky. I found my way to Rajasthan. There was a famine and I couldn't find anything to eat. The cattle had died and even the humans I ate had hardly any flesh on them. So I decided to get back to the zoo. Here at least I get one square meal every day. But you look healthy enough. Why did you come back?'

Replied the fat tiger, 'To start with I was very lucky. I found my way to the government secretariat. I hid myself under a staircase. Every evening as the clerks came out of their offices, I caught and ate one of them. For six months no one noticed anything. Then yesterday I made the mistake of eating the fellow who serves them their morning tea. Then all hell broke loose. They looked for him everywhere and found me hiding under the staircase. They chased me out. So I am back at the zoo. It is safer here.'

☺

This comes from a young entrant to the Indian Administrative Service. His first posting was as a junior assistant to the secretary of the ministry.

One morning, he took some important files to discuss with his boss. After knocking on the door and receiving no reply, he gently pushed open the door to find his senior standing by the window deeply engrossed in his thoughts. He tiptoed out of the room. Since the files were marked 'Immediate', he went back to the secretary's room and, again receiving no reply to the knock, went in. The boss was still standing where he had been and intently looking out of the window. Junior sahib coughed lightly to make his presence known. The secretary turned around and remarked, 'How can this country go forward! For the last one hour I have been watching the workmen on the road. They haven't done a stroke of work.'

Money: Workers earn it, spendthrifts burn it, bankers lend it, forgers fake it, swindlers swindle it, taxes take it, people dying leave it, heirs receive it, thrifty people save it, misers crave it, rich increase it, robbers seize it, gamblers stake it—we could use it.

A politician was asked about his attitude towards whiskey. Here are his candid comments:

'If you mean the demon drink that poisons the mind, pollutes the body and desecrates family life, then I'm against it. But if you mean the elixir of life, the shield against chill, the taxable potion that puts needed funds into public coffers, then I'm for it. This is my position and I'll not compromise.'

Banta: 'If you were offered a chicken from the Congress party and one from the American president, which one would you select?'
Santa: 'The one from the Congress party.'
Banta: 'Because you are a nationalist?'
Santa: 'No, because a bird from the "Hand" is worth two from Bush.'

Question: What should be the thrust of India's foreign policy?
Answer: Chini Kum.

Twenty-five-paise coins have gone off circulation since 30 June 2011. The government feels it can't handle one Anna (Anna Hazare); so there is no need for four Annas.

Then there is the incident narrated in *The Princely India I Knew* by Sir Conrad Corfield about Lady Reading.

Lady Reading seldom lost her viceregal poise and attended every function in spite of failing health, but she had her own sense of humour. One evening, when the viceroy's orchestra was performing during dinner, she enquired the title of the dance tune which was being played. No one could remember. So her ADC was sent to ask the bandmaster.

The conversation at the table changed to another subject during the ADC's absence. He slipped into his seat on return and waited for an opportunity to impart his information. At the next silence, he leant forward to catch Lady Reading's eye and, in a penetrating voice, said, 'I will remember your kisses, Your Excellency, when you have forgotten my name.'

Questions and Answers

Question: How can you drop a raw egg onto a concrete floor without cracking it?
IAS topper: Concrete floors are very hard to crack.

Question: If it took eight men 10 hours to build a wall, how long would it take four men to build it?
UPSC topper: No time at all. It is already built.

Question: If you have three apples and four oranges in one hand and four apples and three oranges in the other hand, what would you have?
UPSC 23rd rank, opted for IFS: Very large hands.

Question: How can a man go eight days without sleep?
Answer: No problem. He sleeps at night.

Tamilian Connection

I confess to my total inability to understand the politics of our southern states. I am sure this is largely due to my inability to pronounce words of Dravidian origin. Linguistically speaking, I draw a line from Pune to Vijayawada. I do not have much difficulty in understanding what goes on in the northern three-quarters of the country. But once the Pune-Vijayawada line is crossed, I am all at sea. I do not suffer from snobbery of any kind. On the contrary, I have a distinct sense of inferiority in dealing with my South Indian friends: their IQs are higher, their minds nimbler, and they are more *Bharatvasi* (Indian) in their culture and their adherence to tradition.

I also find them more attractive than people of the north. What other region of our country can match a Sridevi or a Jaya Prada? Or send to parliament a woman as fair and speech-perfect as Jayalalitha Jayaram?

I belong to the class of semi-literate Punjabis who regard places and persons south of Pune as Madras and Madrasis. Our mental block against the South is entirely due to the tongue-twisting names they have given themselves and their habitats. How can we tackle Bodinayikkanur, Tiruchirapalli, Upptiliyappan, Erachezhiyan, Azagiyasinhar? Dravida Munetra Kazhagam we have got used to; but now we also have a party called Tamizhagar Munnetra Munnani. Our Tamilian brothers and sisters add to our confusion by their convoluted politics. We were told that the Dravida movement launched by Periyar and carried forward by Anna Dural and M.G. Ramachandran was anti-God, anti-Aryan, anti-Hindi, and above all, anti-Brahmin. Now we find the same M.G. Ramachandran's flag being carried aloft by two ladies, both Brahmins—one an Aiyyar, the other, an Iyengar.

Their shifting alliances with other parties make the political scene worse confounded. Their election manifestos read very much alike. To gain women's votes, all of them promise reservation of seats for women in the services; yet in their lists of candidates, there are very few women. It would appear that it is not performance in the political field but on the cinema screen that counts most in Tamil Nadu. The Congress party has sensed this. It is relying heavily on projecting Rajiv Gandhi as a mega film star. It hopes to cash in on his good looks rather than performance as prime minister. His handsomeness may prove to be a winning card with women voters. That's Tamilian democracy for you!

Things are getting bitter,
So, the PM is on twitter.
Will it salvage,
His former image,
And restore his lost glitter?

3
Community Jokes

Stereotypes are one thing; ignorance about other communities can also be very amusing. Let me tell you of a personal experience.

I was staying in King David Hotel, Jerusalem. To most Israelis, India was an unknown country. Very few Indians visited Israel; very few Israelis were earlier allowed to come to India. They had rarely seen a Sikh, and if they saw one, they could not tell whether he was from India or from one of the Arab countries. One evening when I went to the dining room, I was given a table next to an American-Jewish couple on their first visit to their holy land. They gaped at me in disbelief, held whispered consultations with each other and with the waiters. When they could not contain their curiosity anymore, the man turned to me and asked:

Community Jokes

'Sir, can you speak English?'

'Yes, I can,' I replied.

'My wife, Ruth, and I were wondering where you are from and of what faith?'

'I'll give you three guesses,' I replied.

'You wouldn't be Jewish?' ventured his wife.

'No, I am not a Jew,' I replied.

'Don't be silly, how could he be Jewish?' the man snubbed his wife.

'Would you be a Mussalman?'

'No, I am not a Mussalman,' I replied.

The man chewed his cigar and asked, 'A Buddhist?'

'No, I am not even a Buddhist,' I replied.

'I give up, tell us who you are.'

'I am a Sikh,' I replied.

'A Sheikh? Isn't that a Mussalman?'

'Not a Sheikh, not a Mussalman, but a Sikh.'

'I get it,' said the man triumphantly, 'you are from Sikkim.'

Of course jokes based on stereotypes are narrated with great gusto. I will mention some from my collection:

An elderly Punjabi admitted to the intensive care department of a hospital made a request that he should be allowed to take lessons in Urdu. The doctor in charge was very puzzled and asked him the reason why.

'Urdu is the language of angels,' replied the Punjabi. 'If I die I want to be able to converse with all the houris I will meet in paradise.'

'How can you be sure you will go to heaven?' asked the doctor. 'You may go down to hell, then what good will Urdu, which you call the language of angels, be to you?'

'That will be no problem. I am fluent in Punjabi.'

Gorkhas are famous for the discipline they observe in the army and the respect with which they treat their officers.

Once there was a fire in a high-rise building occupied by the army. No sooner had they heard the alarm, a batch of Gorkha jawans ran out with a heavy net to rescue those who jumped down from the upper storeys. Some clerks came down and were saved.

Then their commanding officer leapt from the top floor. The soldiers saw him hurtling down. They dropped the net, sprang to attention and saluted. The colonel was not as lucky as the clerks.

A Sardarji, newly arrived in Calcutta, was invited by his Bengali neighbour to what he thought was to be a bhojan *(feast). He*

ate nothing all day, so he could do justice to rice and macher jhol (fish curry) and rosogollas. He arrived at the appointed time and was regaled with a feast of hymn singing—bhajan!

Sindhis are known both for their sharp practices as well as for their clannishness—they drive hard bargains but also help fellow Sindhis find employment. The following story was told to me by a Sindhi businessman on a visit to Hong Kong.

The businessman wanted to have a silk suit made and went to a Sindhi tailor's shop at the airport which advertised suits made to measure in a couple of hours. The visiting businessman selected the material and asked how much it cost. The tailor replied, 'Sir, seeing you are a fellow Sindhi I will offer you a special price. A suit of this material costs 200 Hong Kong dollars as you can see clearly marked on the label. I charge everyone else $200 but not a fellow Sindhi. I won't ask for $199, not even $180. For you, it will be $170, not a cent more.'

'Why should you lose money on me just because I happen to be a fellow Sindhi,' replied the visitor. 'So what should I offer for this suit? Seventy dollars? That I would to a non-Sindhi brother. I offer you ninety dollars and not a cent less.'

'Okay. That's a deal,' replied the tailor.

4
Sardarji Jokes

Though laughter is the elixir of life—the best tonic in the world to ensure a long and happy life—we are very touchy about a large number of topics. We must not make jokes about God or religion; we must not make jokes about our elders; we must not make jokes about revered figures of our history except those which have been sanctioned by tradition—like for example those of Akbar and Birbal or about Maharaja Ranjit Singh and Akali Phula Singh. Try and crack a joke about Chhatrapati Shivaji within earshot of a Maharashtrian and you'll understand what I mean.

We are equally sensitive about community jokes, which form a rich storehouse of humour of other countries. Although we have lots of proverbs of different castes and subcommunities like Julahas, Naees, Jats, Banias, Marwaris

Sardarji Jokes

and others, we do not think it is right to relate these in the presence of members of those subgroups. Perhaps the largest number of jokes current today are what are known as Sardarji jokes. What is surprising about this genre of jokes is that although most of them are made up by Sardarjis themselves, narrated with great gusto by them and arouse guffaws of healthy laughter; [but] heaven help a non-Sardarji who is foolish enough to take the same liberty in the company of Sardarjis. Sardarjis are a unique combination of a people able to laugh at themselves but totally unable to stand other people laughing at them.

But being a Sardar, let me tell you a few Sardarji jokes.

Once I was travelling from Mumbai to Singapore. A woman sitting in the next seat continued looking at me. I understood that this lady had never seen a Sardar before. Midway in the flight when the tea and snacks were served, I struck a conversation with the lady. Her name was Margarita and she belonged to Spain. During the conversation, she asked, 'What are you?' I replied, 'I am Sikh.' Said the young lady, 'I am sorry. Hope you get well soon.' To this, I replied, 'No dear, I am not sick as that of the body, I am Sikh as of religion.' The lady was very pleased and shook hands with me, and said, 'It is nice meeting you. I am also sick of religion.'

☺

Apparently former President Zail Singh was operated on in the same Texan hospital as his predecessor Sanjiva Reddy. When taken to the operating theatre, the chief surgeon asked our former rashtrapati, 'Are you ready?'

'No I am not Reddy,' replied Gyaniji, 'I am Zail Singh.'

Santa Singh and Banta Singh were always boasting of their parents' achievements to each other.

Santa Singh: 'Have you heard of the Suez Canal?'
Banta Singh: 'Yes, I have.'
Santa Singh: 'Well, my father dug it.'
Banta Singh: 'That's nothing. Have you heard of the Dead Sea?'
Santa Singh: 'Yes, I have.'
Banta Singh: 'Well, my father killed it.'

Banta Singh: 'Er, is that Air India office? Can you tell me how long it takes to fly from Delhi to Bombay?'
Booking clerk: 'Just a minute, sir...'

Banta Singh: 'Okay. Thanks a lot.' *And he hangs up.*

☺

American tourist: 'Where were you born?'
Banta: 'Punjab.'
American: 'Which part?'
Banta: 'What do you mean by "which part"? Oye, my whole body born in Punjab.'

☺

Banto lost her purse in a DTC bus. She lodged an FIR at a police station.

Inspector: 'Madam, where did you put your purse?'
Banto: 'It was a small purse; I kept it in my blouse.'
Inspector: 'It is strange that a thief stole the purse from your blouse and you did not notice it.'
Banto: 'At that time, I did not realize that he was stealing my purse.'

☺

Santa's daughter Pammy was to be married. But as the wedding day got closer, she grew nervous. This was noticed by her mother who asked her the reason.

'It's the thought of going away on a honeymoon with him that's worrying me,' replied Pammy.

'Don't let that bother you,' assured her mother. 'I went on my honeymoon after I got married. So it's no big deal.'

Pammy said, 'Ah, it was all right for you. Tussi papaji naal gaye see (You went with Papaji).'

Two terrorists were driving their Maruti to the spot where they intended to place their bomb. The one in the driver's seat looked very worried. 'Natha, what happens if the bomb we have on the back seat blows up before we get to the site?'

'Not to worry,' replied Natha, 'I have a spare one in my attaché case.'

Two Sardarjis, both students of IIT, Kanpur, were talking about the American astronauts. One said to the other, 'What's the big deal about going to the moon—anybody can go to the moon. We are Sikhs—we'll go directly to the sun.'

'But if we get within thirteen million miles of the sun, we'll melt.'

The first answered, 'So what? We'll go at night.'

Sardarji Jokes

Kakey da Hotel is a very popular eating place in Connaught Circus. It started off as a humble Kakey da Dhaba with stools and charpoys laid out on the pavement, and the tandoor, handis and pateelas *placed in the open. With prosperity the kitchen went into the rear and a dining room was furnished with tables, chairs as well as a washbasin.*

One evening, a patron having finished his meal went to rinse his mouth in the washbasin. He proceeded to do so with great vigour; gargling, spitting 'thooh thooh' and blowing his nose. This ruined the appetites of other diners who protested to the proprietor. Kakaji went to the rinser-spitter and admonished him. 'Haven't you ever eaten in a good hotel before?' he demanded.

'Indeed, I have', replied the errant mouth-rinser. 'I have eaten at the Taj, Maurya, Oberoi, Imperial, Hyatt.'

'What did they say to you when you rinsed your mouth making all these unpleasant sounds?'

'They asked, "You think this is Kakey da Hotel?", and threw me out.'

My friend O.P. Sharma, former additional collector, Bhopal, told me a funny thing.

He said: If we add the Hindi alphabet 'A' before some Hindi words, their meaning becomes negative like: Vishwas—avishwas; shanti—ashanti; kushal—akushal; gyan—agyan; shikshit—ashikshit.

When we add 'A' before the word 'sardar', the new word becomes positive and powerful too: Sardar—asardar.

Santa: Do you know why Dr Manmohan Singh goes to his office only in the afternoon? Why doesn't he go to work in the morning like everyone else?'
Banta: 'It is so simple. Because Manmohan is P.M., not A.M.'

When Indira Gandhi had Giani Zail Singh elected president she began to doubt the wisdom of her choice. She called a cabinet meeting and told them, 'Giani speaks no English. How will he communicate with other heads of states?'

They pondered over the problem and decided that Gianiji should be given an English tutor. 'But only a head of state should teach the head of our state,' was the cabinet consensus.

So a global tender was floated for a head of state to teach Gianiji English. Only Ronald Reagan applied. 'You send him over to the White House for six months and I'll have him speaking English like a Yank,' he wrote.

So Gianiji was flown to Washington and was a house guest of the Reagans. After six months, Indira sent for Rajiv and said, 'Our president has been missing for a long time. You go to Washington, find out how much English he has learnt and bring him back.'

So Rajiv flew to Washington and called on the Reagans at the White House. 'Mr President, I've come to fetch Gianiji and find out how much English you have taught him.'

Reagan replied in rustic Punjabi, 'Iss munday nun angrezee kadee nahin aunee (This lad will never pick up English).'

Have you heard this one about Milkha Singh—the Flying Sikh?

'Are you relaxing?'
'No, I am Milkha Singh.'

Might have heard it half a century ago.

In any case, he wasn't relaxing. He was sleeping soundly in his village home when a thief broke in. He happened to drop something. The crash woke up Milkha. The thief ran. Milkha sprinted, Olympic speed, after him. On the way, he ran into another Sardarji.

'Milkha Singhji, where are you heading for at this pace at this hour of the night?'

'Chasing a thief.'

'A thief? Where is he?'

'Oh, I left him far behind.'

Bet you hadn't heard that before! Ha, ha ha!

Ha, ha, my foot! Tell you a true one.

The H.L. College of Commerce, Ahmedabad, invited me to be their chief guest at the annual prize-giving day. Mona Chinubhai, whose looks have been the talk of the Gujarat capital for many years, extended her hospitality to me. I said 'Yes' to both.

There was another Sardarji on the aircraft. He had a bit of the Flying Sikh in him. Also, he was the first to leap down the Caravelle's tail. The reception committee, consisting of the principal and a bevy of professors, approached him and, without asking any questions, garlanded him. The Sardarji accepted them in good grace. A friend told Mona Chinubhai that they had got the wrong Sardarji. Before they could make up their minds, the garlanded Singhji had triumphantly driven away with his haul of bouquets.

'We Sikhs look alike,' I consoled my crestfallen hosts. 'We have a saying in Punjab: "Natha Singh, Prem Singh—one and the same thing."'

This is a variation of the many jokes about landings on the moon. When Russians had the lead in space travel these were based on the surprise awaiting the first Russian astronaut landing on the moon, e.g. a notice saying 'Kilroy was here', or of a woman astronaut returning pregnant from the moon.

The Sikh version of man's first landing on the moon goes somewhat as follows:

When the American astronaut Neil Armstrong landed on the moon to take the first big step for humanity, he was greeted by a Sardar and his family.

'When on earth did you people get here?' asked the American.

The Sardar replied in Punjabi, 'Aseen taa desh dey batwarey tey 1947 wich itthey aa gaye (We came here after the Partition in 1947).'

5

Ha Ha Honoris Causa

The University of Manila has decided to introduce a three-year course of study in humour. Humour is serious business. It can have a curriculum as varied as any: wit, repartee, calculated insults, epigrams, puns, riddles, limericks, clerihews, shaggy dog stories, bawdy jokes, sick jokes, clean jokes, mother-in-law jokes. And there are jokes about marriage, which are often chauvinistic in tenor, such as:

Getting married is very much like going to a restaurant with friends. You order what you want, then, when you see what the other fellow has, you wish you had ordered that.

At a cocktail party, one woman said to another, 'Aren't you

wearing your wedding ring on the wrong finger?' The other replied, 'Yes, I am. I married the wrong man.'

☺

Man is incomplete until he is married. Then he is really finished.

☺

Marriage is an institution in which a man loses his bachelor degree and the woman gets her master.

☺

Young son: 'Is it true, Dad, that in some parts of the world, a man doesn't know his wife until he marries her?'
Dad: 'That happens in most countries, son.'

☺

Then there was a woman who said: I never knew what real happiness was until I got married, and then it was too late.

☺

A happy marriage is a matter of give and take; the husband gives and the wife takes.

☺

Married life is very frustrating. In the first year of marriage, the man speaks and the woman listens. In the second year, the woman speaks and the man listens. In the third year, they both speak and the neighbours listen.

☺

After a quarrel, a wife said to her husband, 'You know, I was a fool when I married you.' And the husband replied, 'Yes, dear, but I was in love and didn't notice it.'

☺

A man inserted an ad in the classifieds: 'Wife wanted.'

The next day, he received hundreds of letters. They all said the same thing: 'You can have mine.'

☺

A woman marries a man expecting he will change, but he doesn't. A man marries a woman expecting she won't change, and she does!

☺

Ha Ha Honoris Causa

Wife: 'Darling, why do you keep my photo in your wallet?'
Husband: 'That is because whenever I am in trouble, I look at it and feel better.'
Wife: 'You mean to say that my photo has such a soothing effect on you?'
Husband: 'Yes, you are right. When I look at your photo, I console myself that my other problems are not as big as this one!'

As soon as other universities, apart from Manila University, begin to award degrees in humour, you will see that no one will thereafter consider humour a subject for laughter. I hope very much our schools and colleges will introduce humour as a subject of study. Many foreigners have remarked that Indians seldom smile.

The first thing to do is clear our minds about what is humorous. The basis of humour is the puncturing of another person's ego, causing him or her some kind of embarrassment which makes him or her lose his or her dignity. All laughter is at some other person's expense. A man slips on a banana skin and even though his buttocks may be seriously bruised, you burst out laughing. A much-respected citizen is unable to contain the wind in his stomach and farts in public. He cannot thereafter face his fellow citizens and his respect is lost forever. You who enjoy farting in private revel in the other fellow's discomfiture, tell everyone about it and laugh and laugh till tears roll down your cheeks.

Malice is the essence of jest. Jest is an important safety valve to preserve one's sanity against the pressure of accumulated malice.

The following story would fall into the category of jest rather than malice but is amusing nonetheless.

God created a mule and told him, 'You will be a mule, work constantly from dawn to dusk, and carry heavy loads on your back. You will eat grass and lack intelligence. You will live for 50 years.'

The mule answered, 'To live like that for 50 years will be too much. Please, Lord, give me no more than 20 years.' And it was so.

Then God created a dog and told him, 'You will hold vigilance over the dwellings of man to whom you will be the greatest companion. You will eat his table scraps and live for 25 years.'

The dog responded, 'Lord, to live 25 years as a dog like that will be too much. Please, Lord, give me no more than 10 years.' And it was so.

God then created a monkey and told him, 'You will be a monkey. You will swing from tree to tree and act like an idiot. You will be funny, and you will live for 20 years.'

The monkey responded, 'Lord, to live 20 years as the clown of the world will be too much. Please, Lord, give me no more than 10 years.' And it was so.

Finally, God created man and told him, 'You will be the only rational being that walks on the earth. You will use your intelligence to have mastery over other creatures of the world. You will dominate the earth and live for 20 years.'

The man responded, 'Lord, to be a man for only 20 years will be too little. Please, Lord, give me the 30 years the mule refused, the 15 years the dog refused, and the 10 years the monkey refused.' And it was so.

Ever since the grant of that wish man's life goes somewhat like this—he lives the first 20 years as a man enjoying himself without a worry in the world; then he marries and has children; to support them he has to work like a mule and carry the heavy responsibility (load) of his family on his shoulders. This goes on till he is 40. The next 15 years he lives a dog's life guarding his house and eating leftovers after the children have emptied the pantry. Finally, in his old age, he lives the last 10 years as a monkey, entertaining his grandchildren by acting like an idiot. And so it has been ever since.

* * *

Psychologists believe that laughter is necessary to keep one's balance of mind. We are touchy about many things and are quick to take offence. A hearty laugh releases aggressive impulses which, if they remain bottled up inside us, explode in anger and violence. You will notice that people who do not laugh are often constipated with hate. Psychologists also tell us that the ability to see the ridiculous develops very early in a human child. Watch a baby gurgle and chortle, become helpless with laughter when its parents make asinine noises or play peekaboo with it. By the age of seven you can detect whether or not your child will develop into a good raconteur.

The ability to tell a joke is inborn. One child of seven will know how to tell a story with a straight face, how long a pause to make before delivering the punchline. Another will ruin the same story by beginning to laugh while telling it and, by forgetting the all-essential pause to create a sense of expectancy, deliver the punchline in a hurry and so murder the joke. Training in storytelling may improve the child a little, but not very much. Storytellers, like mathematicians, are born, not made.

It stands to reason that humour is as old as humanity itself. Long before we learnt to write we were making fun of each other. As usual, the Greeks were the first people to record different varieties of humour. The earliest recorded joke I have come across is the repartee between an elderly Greek woman driving her herd of asses and a cheeky young man.

'Good morning, mother of asses,' greeted the youngster.
'Good morning, my son,' replied the woman.

We must cultivate a sense of humour and learn to laugh at ourselves. But have no illusions about the price you will have to pay. Laughter and success do not go together. You have to choose between being a VIP and being a jester. Thomas Corwin, a member of the US Congress, put it very succinctly: 'Never make people laugh. If you would succeed in life you must be solemn, solemn as an ass. All the great monuments are built over solemn asses.'

We Indians may have lost our sense of humour but we still have a rich laboratory of materials to work on. Every third Indian is a clown in his own right: self-esteem, immodesty, sanctimoniousness, name-dropping and verbosity make a golden treasury of the ridiculous. We could study all these aspects, channel them into stories and then grant degrees to the more laugh-producing dissertations. We could make a very spectacular start by awarding doctorates even before the courses in humour are launched by conferring on our politicians' degrees of Ha Ha Honoris Causa!

6

The Joys of Farting, and the Pleasure of Pissing

Despite the embarrassment it can cause, I think farting is one of the three great joys of life. First, sex; second, oil rubbed on a scalp full of dandruff; third, a long, satisfying fart. With the onset of middle age I have reversed the order of merit: farting now tops my list of life's pleasures.

The king of farts is the Trumpet—known to our ancestors as *Uttam Paadam*—its noise rendered as *phadakaam*. It is an act of will, it is proclamatory, it is masculine. It has much sound, little smell. The louder, the less odorous. My friend, the bald, beady-eyed photographer who has done considerable research on the subject is an exponent of the Trumpet. He is of the considered opinion that the Trumpet can only be produced by people who restrict their diet to fresh fruits and non-fibrous vegetables grown above the ground. Such food is sattvic—pure. Poultry, fish and meat, though nourishing, are of the secondary rajas category. Spices, stale food like pickles, preserves and chutneys; vegetables which grow underground like potatoes, radishes, carrots and garlic, or are attached to the earth like onions, cabbages, turnips and cauliflowers are definitely tamas. My photographer friend demonstrated the Trumpet by consuming a succulent watermelon on an empty stomach. An hour later he was airborne like a jet plane.

Second in the order of farts is the Shehnai—our ancestors also give it a secondary status—*Madhyamaa*—and its sound is rendered as *thain, thain*. I prefer to compare it to the *shehnai*, a wind instrument made famous by the maestro Ustaad Bismillah Khan of Varanasi. Like the Trumpet, the Shehnai is also an act of will and may be produced by a simple shift in position or gentle pressure on the paunch. It differs from the Trumpet in its softer tone and longer duration. The opening notes of a Scottish bagpipe sound very much like it—*pheenh*.

The third variety is the Scraper which makes a sound like a squelch of uncured leather or the rustling of old parchment. It is, in fact, not one but a succession of little farts—*pirt, pirt, pirt, pirt*. The Scraper is a by-product of eating too much of tamasic food. It is also a phenomenon of rectal muscles softened by age.

The fourth is the Tabla. It proclaims itself with a single *phut* like a tap on a bongo drum. The Tabla is its own master as it escapes without the host's consent causing him or her deep embarrassment if they happen to be in company.

The fifth is the noiseless stink bomb, the Phuskin. Since it is unspoken it is best suited to be planted on a neighbour as a secret gift—*gupta daan*. The donor can assume a 'not-I' look on his face or hold his nostrils and turn towards someone else with an accusing look. But he must heed the Japanese saying: 'He who talks is the one who farted.' If you have let off a stinking *gupta daan*, let others guess the identity of the benefactor.

Nations have different attitudes towards farting. The Europeans and Americans are quite shameless about it. It is a part of their Greek inheritance. Niarchos (first century, AD) extolled the virtues of farting any time wind built up in the belly:

If blocked, a fart can kill a man;
If let escape, a fart can sing
Health-giving songs; farts kill and save.
A fart is a powerful king.

Niarchos knew the difference between a noiseless stink bomb and the audible varieties of wind-breaking. To wit:

The Joys of Farting, and the Pleasure of Pissing

Does Henry sigh, or does he fart?
His breath is strong from either part.

Exhortations to the fart are also found in contemporary English literature:

Men of letters ere we part
Tell me why you never fart?
Never fart? Dear Miss Bright,
I do not need to fart, I write.

Although white races eat black rajas food which does not produce much wind, when they have it, they release it in company with total unconcern for propriety. This is particularly revolting in the case of the wine-drinkers making a *gupta daan*: Wind produced by wine is singularly stenchful. The ultimate in white people's vulgarity was a Frenchman who displayed his fart-power on stage. He had a slit made in the back of his trousers and for a small wager would blow out a candle placed three feet from his posterior.

If the whites are disgusting, the Indians are not much better. Indians treat farting as a topic of jest. Since they eat highly spiced tamasic foods, they are the world's champion farters and have much occasion to laugh at each other.

Once, a minister of cabinet recording a talk for the External Services of All India Radio let out a Trumpet.

The talk had to be rerecorded. However, when the time came, by mistake the original recording was put on the air. It gave an Indian the unique distinction of having his fart heard around the world. The *Guinness Book of Records*, please note.

For an unrelenting attitude towards farting, the palm must be given to the Persians and the Arabs. There is a tale told of a young Iranian who broke wind in a *mehfil* (gathering). He was so overcome with remorse that he left the town. After many years in self-imposed exile he returned home hoping that his small misdemeanour would have been forgotten. Naming himself, he asked some boys to direct him to his old home. 'You mean the home of so-and-so, the farter?' demanded the urchins. The poor man went back into exile.

The first prize for courtesy extended to farters goes to Sufi Abdul Rahman Hatam Ibn Unwan al-assam of Balkh, known for reasons of his noble attitude to farting as Hatam the Deaf. It is said that while he was explaining a matter of some theological import to an old woman, the lady farted. The saintly Sufi raised his voice and said, 'Speak louder, I am hard of hearing.' And for the 15 long years that the woman continued to live, Hatam pretended to be hard of hearing and suffered people shouting in his ears. Hatam the Deaf is the patron saint of embarrassed farters.

* * *

The Joys of Farting, and the Pleasure of Pissing

There is something about the wall

The joy of pissing against a wall for a male is perhaps not equal to the joy of farting but enjoyable nonetheless. What a lamp post is to a dog, a wall is to the Indian male. The block of apartments I live in has a long wall. It demarcates our block from the main throughfare and a bus stand. Every bus disgorges dozens of passengers who quickly divide themselves between paan-chewers and pissers. One lot cluster around the paanwallah's booth; the other line themselves against the wall, turn their beatific gazes heavenwards and unzip their trousers. They make little noise but a lot of stink.

If I were a Mughal prince living in Mughal times, I would practise archery on their privates. However, living in an epoch of democracy wherein the nauseous effluent has attained the status of amrit, all I can do is to grumble. I like fountains but have strong views about humans spouting water as and where it pleases them. To prevent further fouling of our environment an iron railing was put a yard removed from the wall. I do not think the railing will daunt any pissers: au contraire, I expect the eruption of a new sport to be named 'hit-the-wall'. Only the middle-aged or those with enlarged prostrates may be daunted by the distance. However, as the old lady said as she pissed in the sea, every little bit helps.

Let me tell you that the only way to prevent people

from pissing is to put up pictures of gods and goddesses at strategic points. We are a superstitious people and would rather piss in our pants than insult our deities.

I canalize my wrath against public urinators by delving into the literature on the subject. Apparently the word piss was quite respectable and used as a synonym for urine because of its echoic-onomatopoeic quality of sound. After AD 1760, the word came to be associated with drunkenness, bragging and sycophancy. A pub became a piss factory (a pub in a London suburb was named The Piss-Pot); to be drunk was to be pissed; or so drunk as to open a shirt collar to piss; gin mixed with hot water came to be known as piss-quick. A braggart became one who pissed more than he drank or a piss-fire because he talked as if he could put out a conflagration by urinating on it. A flatterer was one who pissed down one's back. Something that was never likely to happen came to be known as goose pissing. However, the most appropriate use of the term could mean both generosity as well as niggardliness: to piss on a nettle was to be miserly, to piss money against a wall was to indulge in squandermania. And so on.

I am not sure whether the remark attributed to Clemenceau about Winston Churchill's oratory was meant as a compliment or otherwise. He said, 'Ah! *Si je pouvais pisser comme il parle* (I wish I could piss the way that man talks).'

7
Nose-picking

It is a nauseating habit most of us indulge in, when no one is looking. Tolstoy was forthright in his condemnation: 'People who pick their noses and dispose of the pickings on the undersides of the dinner table are not likely ever to see God.'

So few of us are likely to be let in the Pearly Gates and have darshan of the Almighty. Charles Darwin, author of *The Origin of Species*, found this one distinguishing factor between us and our simian cousins. 'Monkeys do not pick their noses,' he wrote. 'This is about the only disgusting personal human habit at which they are not also adept.'

Who in the world would have thought of writing a book on the subject except an American! So one has—a Yank by the name of Donald Wetzel who wrote *The Nose Pickers' Guide* (Ivory Tower Publishing Co.)

A new word you may like to add to your vocabulary is 'booger'. It is the stuff you extract out of your nostrils. They are of two kinds: dry boogers and wet boogers. Whatever kind they be, you instinctively try to stick them on the sides of the chair you are sitting on, or under the table. If you happen to be out on a walk, you stick them to the sides of your trousers. Beware of depositing them on your bed headrest because the king of shrinks, Sigmund Freud, declared that 'People who put their nose pickings on the pillow case are sick.'

Donald Wetzel has drawn a list of many varieties of boogers. In the dry variety are marble, buckshot, black hole, dry hairy (firmly attached to a large hair in the nostril), smoky bear and pygmy.

Then there is the phantom which does not really exist except in your imagination and you go on probing for it in your nostrils endlessly till somebody screams at you to stop. There is also a bastard booger which refuses to be moulded into a disposable shape and sticks to your finger no matter how much you try to get rid of it. Similarly, wet boogers have many subspecies: fish-eye, pizza, elastic, chicken turd, etc.

Two aspects of nose-picking should be noticed. First is that few people dig for them in their nostrils with

Nose-picking

handkerchiefs. Most people enjoy the exercise using only their index fingers. Oscar Wilde wrote, 'Show me a man who picks his nose with his pinky and I'll show you a man with a nose like a rabbit.'

The other noticeable aspect is that the habit of nose-picking is far more prevalent among men than women. Queen Victoria remarked, 'If one would remain a lady or gentleman, one must thoroughly wash one's hands after picking one's nose.' Her Britannic Majesty was not a nose-picker and was not amused if she caught any of her courtiers probing their nostrils with their fingers.

8
Name-dropping

My other weakness is supposed to be name-dropping. I never object to anyone calling me names or making fun of me. I believe in Burn's dictum to 'see ourselves as others see us'. Many of my readers see me as a name-dropper and a poseur. P.S. Ranganathan of New Delhi has parodied what he thinks I would have written on the deaths of Tagore, Marilyn Monroe and Karl Marx.

The obit on the poet reads as follows:

It was a rainy Sunday morning when I had the opportunity to meet the Nobel Prize winner. Tagore was at a seaside resort in Switzerland, the charming landlocked country of Europe. I was just returning after a two-month holiday-cum-research tour of Polynesia, Hawaii and Las Vegas. I was working on a novel for my publishers, Tom, Dick and Harry, London.

Name-dropping

This novel was also to be published in America by Fung, Wag and Kneel Inc, New York.

I had earlier phoned Tagore for an appointment. 'Sunday, 7.30. Will it suit you?' he asked in a clear voice. 'Oh anything will suit me except my suits stitched in India,' I said. There was hearty laughter at the other end of the phone. Surely, Tagore was a man with a high sense of humour!

When I went on the appointed day, I was slightly late—to be exact, by about 8 hours. Tagore received me at the porch and offered me nimbu-de joiuce, *a delicious drink (certainly I did not expect the poet to offer me Scotch). For the next 40 minutes we discussed the current literary trends. I was then vaguely planning a novel, later to be titled* A Train to Pakistan *(published by Hind Pocket Books or Orient Paperbacks or Pearl Publications. I don't exactly remember the name of the publisher, which is not quite material. The book is priced at `4, which is quite material).*

Tagore asked me what I was doing. 'Nothing of importance,' I said. 'Oh, you Sardarjis are modest to a fault. With your remarkable talent, whatever you do will be important and will certainly make a great impact on the minds of intellectuals. Now, since we are alone, I can tell you this. Your writings are quite outstanding and you are sure to be awarded the Nobel Prize.'

Tagore was a great soul with a great heart. He is gone. I only wish that his statement comes true.

About Miss Monroe, the parody reads as follows:

Marilyn had a soft corner for me. It was just by chance I was seated next to her in a Pan Am jet from New York to London.

'Mr Khushwant, I presume. I am Marilyn Monroe,' she introduced herself. 'Your name is familiar. But I am unable to place you,' I said hesitatingly. 'You must have seen a naked picture of a Hollywood actress in Life. It was mine,' she said.

Then I remembered.

And Karl Marx:

An outstanding thinker and a remarkable writer who was fascinated by my writings. In fact he told a common friend of ours—why should I withhold his name, he was Winston Churchill—well, Marx was telling Winston that he was keen to translate my novel into Russian. Winny—that was how I used to address him—later told me this when we met at Buckingham Palace for a party. I was thrilled by this piece of news but I had to politely decline the offer since another friend of mine was already at the job. If my readers would not say I am dropping names, I can say that the friend was no other person than Tolstoy.

This is what one 'K' can write about another 'K' in this moment of great anguish.

If this be the truth about me, it is time for me to take an overdose of barbiturates.

9

How to Appear Learned Without Learning

Easy! Get a book of quotations, mug up a few lines of the Gita, Koran and the Granth, sprinkle your speech or essay with these borrowed flowers and you've made it. There is an unwritten convention in our country that anyone who quotes Kalidas or Saadi will thereafter be known as a Sanskrit or a Persian scholar. Nothing is more honoris causa. I have exploited the half-a-dozen lines from the Gita that I have memorized to great advantage.

To those who would like to emulate my example to attain 'instant scholarship', I can recommend an excellent publication—*Political Concepts in Ancient India* by P.K. Chaudhuri. It is a lexicon of Sanskrit terminology on political topics. To start with, use *dandaniti* instead of politics and you will have passed your prelims. If your opinion is solicited on our present state of leaderless democracy, instead of floundering around to find appropriate words in English, describe it as *arajaka*—hallowed by the Ramayana and the Mahabharata to describe Aryavarta at times when it was without a ruler. If you are eager to make your number with Atal Bihari, you can tell him the derivation of his surname, *Vajpeya*—a rite performed by a king prior to his consecration. Atal Bihari may already be aware of this. So indulge in a bit of *guna samkirtana* (flattery) by telling him that a *Vajpeya* rite will raise his status from a simple mantri to a *samrat* (emperor).

There are words in Chaudhuri's dictionary which will come in handy when denouncing people you do not like. I have already substituted one word of English that I often use for a more mouthful Sanskrit equivalent. Hereafter, every bastard I meet will be a *gudhajaputra*. However, I am a little foxed by Manu's definition: 'Son born to woman by a man other than her husband through *secret union*.' O great lawgiver! Pray tell us, how does a married woman cohabit with a stranger except through secret union?

* * *

The need to be politically correct can be quite amusing.

The opening formula for letters, 'Dear Sir or Madam',

should hereafter read 'Dear Madam or Sir or whatever the case may be', otherwise you may be exposed to the charge of being anti-feminist. So the Equal Opportunities Committee of London's Hackney Council has opined. It warns men to be more careful in their choice of words pertaining to females of their species. Before putting pen to paper they should ask themselves: 'Are women being excluded, trivialized, patronized, stereotyped or made fun of?' Examples of words which when converted to the feminine gender might offend feminine susceptibilities are appended: dustman must not be dustwoman but a 'refuse operative'; foreman not a forewoman but 'supervisor'; and housewife, 'consumer-shopper'. Similar verbal reforms are proposed for disabled persons: a sightless person must not be called blind but 'visually handicapped'; and if he or she is one-eyed, as 'suffering from partially visual handicap'.

In Shakespeare's time, a cobbler had been elevated to the status of 'a surgeon unto men's shoes'. In my time, I have known a cook designated 'canteen officer'; dhobi, a 'launderer'; and a sweeper, a 'garbage remover'. How does change in the nomenclature change the drudgery of the occupation or assuage the feelings of the deprived?

10

Talking Shop

I am never irked by people of the same profession exchanging experiences. They are seldom too technical for the layman and soon come down to true anecdotes. Thus, an architect may tell you of problems created by wives of their clients regarding the exact location of the loo or the washbasin; a doctor of his cussed patients. Quite understandably, lawyers have the largest repertoire of experience to draw from: their clients' tribulations, exchange with witnesses in the witness box, repartee with judges. The bar association of any town is a veritable anecdote-producing factory.

In my brief and somewhat briefless career as an advocate at the Lahore High Court there was nothing I enjoyed more than an evening with other lawyers recounting their day's experiences. I recall an exchange between Lata Bhagat Ram

Puri, then leader of the Bar, and a very irate English judge. Every point made by Puri was contemptuously dismissed with one word—'nonsense'. Then Puri's patience ran out and he rasped, 'Nothing but nonsense seems to come out of your Lordship's mouth this morning.'

An encounter with a female witness still rankles in my mind. I was appearing for the prosecution in a murder case where the accused's wife, a prostitute, was giving evidence of alibi to the effect that her husband was with her in her house at the time of the murder. Their home was some distance from the brothel where the lady carried on her business and where the murder had taken place at night—the usual working hour in her profession. I proceeded to cross-examine her, 'How is it that you were not at your place of business that night?'

'I practise my profession during the daytime,' she replied somewhat tartly.

'How can that be? Don't your patrons seek you at hours usual in the profession?'

'Oh, no, Sir,' she replied coquettishly. 'Only goondas, badmashes and other lowly types visit brothels at night. Respectable gentlemen like yourself come in daytime.'

11

Nick to the Name

I have mentioned bawdy jokes earlier. Here is an example.

There was a man who lost all his children soon after they were born. He consulted a learned pandit who advised him that he should give his children to come ugly names so that God (who presumably doesn't mouth obscenities) would not send for them. Following the wise man's advice the man named his next son after the male genital, the daughter who followed after the female genital, and being a whole-hogger, named the kid his goat had delivered 'Buttocks'. It worked. The three attained puberty in good health. It is not recorded how the two humans with these peculiar names fared in social circles.

But the story reaches its bawdy climax at the nuptials of

the girl and her mother's pleading with her son-in-law to be considerate towards her child (named you know what). The irate, un-understanding son-in-law stomps out of the house, and his father-in-law runs after him pleading that he was as dear to him as his own son (you know who) and if he came back he would slaughter (the Hindi word is maro*) the goat-kid to feast him.*

There is a moral behind this bawdy tale: only he or she who has to live with it should have the right to choose their name. Since a child has to be called something, the parents may give it a temporary label which its incumbent should be entitled to shed as it sheds its milk teeth and choose another which it fancies.

* * *

A problem is also posed by nicknames. These are given unasked and are more often than not meant to hurt. Imagine the agony of an obese child being called Bessie or Billy Bunter, Fatso or Motu! Or of a thin child being called Skinny! A long-nosed one being a Concorde! A thick-lipped being a Lipso. Often nicknames do not allude to physical features but are mutilations of the real name. For some reason I was nicknamed Shali which I did not mind too much. But when it came to be rhymed—*Shali Shooli*

Bagh ki Mooli (radish in the garden)—I minded it very much. For some mysterious reason Shali died out, and I was re-nicknamed Khusrau which I do not mind too much. But when Khusrau had its tail docked and I was labelled Khusra (eunuch) I minded it very much. Now I read of a poor Indian girl in England with a nice name like Suneeta being nicknamed Snot-eater.

The vicissitudes through which nicknames pass are infinite. A publication, *Nicknames: Their Origin & Social Consequences*, mentions a child nicknamed Polly (Scots for chubby) successively being re-nicknamed Pearshape, Persia, Iran, Irene, Irebus and finally, Bus. How true was Hazlitt in his opinion that a nickname is the hardest stone that the Devil can throw at a man! But seldom do nicknames pursue their bearers into adult life.

Then we design all kinds of euphemisms to cover up unpleasant truths. A blind man is a Nainsukh, Surdas, Soorma, or Lakhnetra (with 100,000 eyes). Plutarch mentions that this was a common practice in ancient Athens where a harlot was described as a companion, tax as a donation, a dungeon as a chamber.

Another right that should be granted to all mankind is to change their names to suit the country they happen to be in. I recall an embarrassing encounter with a distinguished Swede, a Mr Lund (very common name in Scandinavia)

Nick to the Name

who was due to visit India. After a few drinks I got the courage to tell him that he should not be upset if northern Indians smiled or sniggered at being introduced to him and explained what his name meant in Hindustani. He was most amused and told me that he had not long before escorted an Indian lady called Miss Das and had to introduce her to various audiences.

'Why should that have embarrassed you?' I asked him.

'Because in Swedish the word "dass" means shit,' replied Mr Lund.

* * *

Getting back to bawdy jokes, family planning has resulted in a plethora of jokes, some very risqué, others less so.

A rich lady had a family of four children, all of whom turned out to be very bright. She was always boasting of their records at school and was sure when they grew up they would bring credit to India. I asked her somewhat sarcastically if she had ever heard of the family planning slogan—*hum do humaarey do*. 'Yes', she replied somewhat haughtily, 'that is for the *aira gaira* (hoi polloi), not for people like us who have highly intelligent children and can afford to give them the best of education.'

'In that case, why don't you have five more and give India another nau ratans (nine gems)?'

She ignored my sarcasm and replied, 'I have just read a book on population statistics. It says that every fifth child born in the world is a Chinese.'

Choudhary Nar Singh was a famous 'pracharak' right from the days of Chhotu Ram, revenue minister of erstwhile Punjab. Later, Bansi Lal made him in charge of the family planning campaign during the Emergency days. One day, Nar Singh came to our village chaupal *and started delivering a lecture on the merits of family planning to a gathering of 200 persons.*

One boy got up and asked, 'Tauji, it is learnt that the physical prowess of the man gets diminished after the operation. Is it true?'

Nar Singh retorted promptly, 'Bhai chhorey, *during the operation it is only the cultivator that is taken off. The tractor ploughs the land as fast as ever.' The whole gathering burst into peals of laughter and the function ended on a happy note.*

12

English – Vinglish

From the number of letters I receive, it would appear that linguistic bloomers are a very popular form of humour. Most of us who are anglicized wogs switch from our native languages to English, interspersing each with words from the other. Even the uneducated make free use of English words. I heard a qawwali singer complain that because of her inattentive audience, 'Mood *kharab ho gaya.*'

A labourer reprimanded the foreman, '*Mere kaam mein* interfere *mat karo.*' And I hear the word 'bore' in almost all Indian languages.

Then there is the mauling of foreign words. A lady reluctant to give up a seat she had occupied proclaimed, 'I am not *nicling* from here.' Mir Pandu Chintamani of Bombay sent a report conveyed by the guard of a train in which the lights were on the blink. It read: *'Bijlee is bajanging...if any haraj maraj ho gaga*, guard is not *jumevar'*.

I don't believe the next one but it is one of my favourites:

A minister for housing (name not disclosed for fear of causing hatred, ridicule or contempt) was presiding over a committee considering plans for building urinals. The plans were examined and passed. The honourable minister made the concluding address: 'Gentlemen, now that we have sanctioned plans for the construction of urinals, it is only appropriate that we should take up the scheme for raising arsenals.'

Brown sahibs have lots of fun spotting grammar and spelling bloomers on hoardings, ads and brochures put out by their countrymen whose command over English is not as good as theirs.

Noted on a signboard in Chandigarh: 'Singh's Chicken, Fully Air-conditioned'.

A young lady went to a hospital and told the receptionist that she wished to see an upturn.

'You mean an intern, don't you dear?' asked the kindly nurse.

'Well, whatever you call it, I want a contamination,' replied the girl.

'You mean examination,' corrected the nurse.

'Maybe so,' allowed the girl. 'I want to go to the fraternity ward.'

'Maternity ward,' said the nurse with a slight smile.

'Look,' insisted the girl, 'I don't know much about big words, but I do know that I haven't demonstrated for two months, and I think I am stagnant.'

The teacher of a primary school in Punjab advised his class in the best traditions of Punjabi English: 'When you are empty meet me behind the class.'

On another occasion he told them if they had any question to ask: 'Stand your hand.'

Once when he had some problem with his eyes, he sent an application to the principal asking for leave: 'Sir, I cannot come to school because my eyes have come. I will report for duty when they go.'

A firm which undertakes to destroy vermin has sent me its terms of contract. If its ability to kill pests is as great as its ability to kill the English bhasha then I can strongly commend it. Instructions are:

On Humour

(1) *Before start the work empted every thing.*
(2) *In the bed Room Cuboards to be empted.*
(4) *When the Job is started, nobody can stay inside after fumigation to keep two hours in the Flat*
(5) *After open the Flat only clean with dry cloth.*

Much funnier are linguistic faux pas committed by those who assume familiarity with a lingo without really knowing it. I recall an angry letter written by a teacher of English to the chairman of her school:

'Dear Sir, I wish to resignate...'

I have been toying with the idea of writing a learned article on a new language which is gaining currency in the well-to-do urban society of India. I have been deterred from the task by two reasons. One is that I am incapable of writing anything very learned. And the other is that I am not sure how to describe this language except in the classical *neti neti* (not this, not this). It is not Hobson-Jobson or the Anglo-Indian slang spoken by the Poonah Sahebs of yesteryears. It is not

English-Vinglish

Babu English, nor the Indo-Anglian of the Mulk Raj Anand school, not even the hotchpotch spoken by the public school smarties and their female counterparts from the convents.

What then is it? I can only offer samples from the writings of the two chief priestesses of this linguistic cult: Devyani Chaubal of *Star and Style* and Shobha Rajadhyaksha (Kilachand) of *Stardust*—both, in their own lingo, *philmi phemales*. When Devyani first *maroed* this bhasha, I was at once *maha* charmed as well as *maha* scandalized. I asked her where she had picked up this language. 'I *banoed* it myself,' she said, 'no *nakal bazi*. Now every *altu faltu* fellow is *nakal maroing* me. There is no *insaf* in this world, no!'

Meanwhile, a lot of work is being done on Amerenglish. Anyone who has spent any time in England and the United States will understand the import of Bernard Shaw's quip about them being two countries divided by a common tongue. Not only have the two peoples invented different words for the same things, the same word can have an entirely different meaning on either side of the Atlantic.

Surprisingly, it is the Americans who are more prudish in their choice of words than the English. Do you know that the grease nipple of a car becomes a grease fitting in the US? The most popular example of the linguistic divide is the word 'fanny'—in the United States it refers to the female posterior (kiss my fanny!), in England, to the frontage. Then there is the innocent feline—pussy. In England it retains its virgin purity unsullied as a kitten. You can caress an English girl's pussy without in any way appearing too bold. But don't try it in the United States.

* * *

An American friend, Leonard J. Baldgya of the US embassy, has sent a short compilation of items picked up by American students in different parts of Europe. They make as good reading as our Hindlish.

- In a Bucharest hotel lobby: *The lift is being fixed for the next day. During that time we regret that you will be unbearable.*
- In a Belgrade hotel elevator: *To move the cabin, push button for wishing floor. If the cabin should enter more persons, each one should press a number of wishing floor. Driving is then going alphabetically by national order.*
- In a hotel in Athens: *Visitors are expected to complain at the office between the hours of 9 and 11 a.m. daily.*
- In a Japanese hotel: *You are invited to take advantage of the chambermaid.*
- In the lobby of a Moscow hotel across from a Russian

Orthodox monastery: *You are welcome to visit the cemetery where famous Russian composers, artists and writers are buried daily except Thursday.*
- In an Austrian hotel catering to skiers: *Not to perambulate the corridors in the hours of repose in the boots of ascension.*
- On the menu of a Polish hotel: *Salad a firm's own make; limpid red beet soup with cheesy dumplings in the form of a finger; roasted duck let loose; beef rashers beaten up in the country people's fashion.*
- In a Bangkok dry-cleaner's shop: *Drop your trousers here for best results.*
- Outside a Paris dress shop: *Dresses for streetwalking.*
- Outside a Hong Kong dress shop: *Ladies have fits upstairs.*
- In an advertisement by a Hong Kong dentist: *Teeth extracted by the latest Methodists.*
- In a Czechoslovakian tourist agency: *Take one of our horse-driven city tours—we guarantee no miscarriages.*
- Detour sign in Kyushi, Japan: *Stop—drive sideways.*
- In a Swiss mountain inn: *Special today—no ice cream.*
- In a Bangkok temple: *It is forbidden to enter a woman, even a foreigner, if dressed as a man.*
- In a Tokyo bar: *Special cocktail for the ladies with nuts.*
- In a Copenhagen airline office: *We take your bags*

and send them in all directions.

- In a Rome laundry: *Ladies, leave your clothes here and spend the afternoon having a good time.*
- A translated sentence from a Russian chess book: *A lot of water has been passed under the bridge since this variation has been played.*
- In a Rhodes tailor shop: *Order your summers suit. Because is big rush we will execute customers in strict rotation.*
- In an East African newspaper: *A new swimming pool is rapidly taking shape since the contractors have thrown in the bulk of their workers.*
- Advertisement for donkey rides in Thailand: *Would you like to ride on your own ass?*
- In the window of a Swedish furrier: *Fur coats made for ladies from their own skin.*
- Two signs from a Majorcan shop entrance: *English well talking. Here speeching American.*
- From a brochure of a car rental firm in Tokyo: *When passenger of foot heave in sight, tootle the horn. Trumpet him melodiously at first, but if he still obstacles your passage then tootle him with vigour.*

English-Vinglish

A Polish man moved from Poland to the United States of America and married an American girl. Although his English was far from being perfect, they got along very well.

Then one day, he rushed to a lawyer's office and asked the lawyer if he could arrange a divorce for him. The lawyer asked him the following questions:

'Have you any ground?'

'Yes, an acre-and-a-half and a nice little home.'

'No, I mean what is the foundation of this case?'

'It is made of concrete.'

'I don't think you understand. Does either of you have a real grudge?'

'No, we have a carport.'

'I mean, what are your relations like?'

'All my relations stay in Poland.'

'Is there any infidelity in your marriage?'

'We have a high-fidelity stereo and a good DVD player.'

'Is your wife a nagger?'

'No, she's white.'

'Why do you want this divorce?'

'My wife is going to poison me. She buy a bottle at drugstore and put it on shelf in bathroom. I can read and it says, "Polish remover".'

Trying to show off familiarity with foreign languages can land you in difficulties.

There is the well-known case of a British minister on a visit to Moscow who in order to please his hosts mugged up a short speech in Russian. On his way to the banquet he realized he did not know the Russian for 'ladies and gentlemen'. He stopped his car near a public lavatory and took down the Russian equivalent. His speech did not get the kind of applause he expected. Afterwards, he asked one of his colleagues what had gone wrong. The colleague replied, 'Your speech was excellent. But why did you have to start with "Male and female urinals"?'

The sound of words often causes confusion in simple minds.

A semi-literate but rich businessman intending to make a bequest to a co-educational institution was dissuaded from doing so by one who wanted the money for his own boys' school. 'Do you know that in the co-ed school boys and girls share the same curriculum?' he asked the donor. 'Moreover they matriculate together.' To drive the point home, he added, 'And worse than that they spend most of their time in seminars.' The bequest was never made.

At times several words telescoped into one more effectively convey their meaning than when used separately. One example I can think of is Robert Lavher's description of congestion on the road: 'The rush hour traffic I'd just as soon miss when carafetercarrismovinglike this.' I thought of something similar to describe the rush hour in our cities; it is bumpertobumpertobumperwithabump.'

* * *

You have to be a master of words to mix flattery with satire. Our ancestors knew the art better than we. Badauni in his *Mantakhab* records some incidents when recipients of rewards were able to combine their disappointment with the gift with flattery for the emperor in the hope of receiving more.

One was the poet Anwari who was presented with an old horse which gave up the ghost on the very night it had been delivered at Anwari's home. Next morning, the poet came to court on foot. 'What happened to the horse we presented you yesterday?' asked the emperor.

Replied the poet, 'It was so fleet-footed that in one night it traversed the distance from the earth to heaven.'

The rapidly changing world ushers in new words. Ecology has been much in vogue in recent years. Apparently our forefathers being closer to the wordless apes had similar problems which they were unable to define. Archaeological excavations prove this, hence Arcology—ecological considerations unearthed by archaeology. Since pornography so obsesses our minds we have Pornesta—the mental condition of one who cannot see the pornographic in his everyday surroundings. Sovexporn for the USSR's Porn Export Agency (presumably on the popularity of their sexy wench Octobrina). And press people who specialize on the subject will hereafter be designated Pornospondents.

13

Irony, Satire and Witty Terminology

*I*rony and satire is also a form of humour. Here are some personal anecdotes of this genre:

When I was in college, my friend Bharat Ram wore the coarsest khadi and exhorted all of us to do the same. He inherited a vast complex of textile mills but that did not lessen his zeal for the hand-spun cloth. He would go to work in an air-conditioned Jaguar. Every day he took one hour off from work to sit on a beautiful Persian carpet and in the midst of the humming of a thousand power looms, solemnly ply his Amber charkha. He did not think there was anything incongruous about it. I thought it was very funny.

After Independence I served for some years in India House in London. At first my boss Krishna Menon used to come to office by bus and, instead of occupying a huge mansion in Millionaires Row meant for the High Commissioner, slept in a small room attached to his office. I was deeply impressed because I felt that this was as Gandhiji would have liked all Indians, however rich and well-placed, to live. However, a few months after assuming office he bought an enormous Rolls-Royce and a fleet of Austin Princess cars for his own use and the use of his senior aides. He said that the Rolls-Royce and the Austins were necessary to maintain the prestige of India. I thought it very funny.

Back in Delhi I chanced to see a circular sent by then Prime Minister Nehru drawing attention to public criticism of the ostentatious style of living of many senior civil servants. It was based on a note written by R.K. Nehru, then foreign secretary, on the advisability of dividing three-acre bungalows allotted to the top brass, careful use of official cars and the need to cut down generally on living expenses. At the time R.K. Nehru rode a Cadillac and the bill for refurnishing his three-acre house had drawn adverse comment in the press. I thought that note was very funny.

A few weeks ago a number of members of parliament were invited by Air India for a free ride to New York and back. These gentlemen had won their elections by persuading voters that they were for the poor and would soon be *hataoing garibi*. Now they protested to Air India that travelling

Irony, Satire and Witty Terminology

economy class was a slight to their dignity and they should be provided first-class travel. I think this very funny.

Our former *Rashtrapati* Shri V. V. Giri was a trade union man fighting for the rights of the poor exploited workers. We thought, as the head of the republic, he would demonstrate how greatness, as with Gandhiji, goes better with simple living than with grandeur. However, he lived in viceregal grandeur in his 133-acre palace and gardens with almost 2,000 servants to cater for his needs as our *rashtrapati*. Besides the Lutyens Bhavan, he had other residences in Simla and Hyderabad and a Swiss-made air-conditioned railway saloon to carry him about. And then a six-door Mercedes-Benz to escort VIPs who visited him! Our own humbler Ambassadors, Fiats and Heralds would not do. The former prime minister dismissed all this as of little consequence. Now I think it is a waste of time to think such thoughts.

An anonymous letter I received from Islamabad containing an unsigned poem entitled, 'A User's Guide to Indian Causology', I found extremely witty and biting in its satire. I reproduce it in full for Indian readers:

On Humour

When the monsoon fails and the sun drums down
On the parched Gangetic plain
And the tanks dry up and dust storms blow
Where once were fields of grain.
When hunger stalks each village hut
And famine grips the land,
It isn't Mother Nature's fault
It is the Foreign Hand!
For this is India, you see,
Not Germany or France,
And nothing here is blamed on God,
Much less on quirky chance.
Here evil has a fingered form
Both alien and planned.
It is the Foreign Hand!
When Hindu lads hack Sikhs to death
In peaceful Delhi town.
When Rajiv's corns are acting up
Or the Bombay bourse goes down,
When the pesky little Nepalese
Insist on things like borders.
When once-tame Tamil Tigers balk
At taking South Block orders.
The reasons for this mischief
I think you'll understand

Irony, Satire and Witty Terminology

It's those meddling foreign digits
It is the Foreign Hand!
So when you're in a Delhi lift
Beside a buxom dame
And you give in to the natural urge
To pinch her husky frame,
Confront her adamantine glare
With a visage mildly bland,
And say: 'It wasn't me, my dear,
It was the Foreign Hand!'

Witty Terminology

The following answers were given by an applicant for admission to a medical college:

- *antibody—against everyone*
- *artery—the study of fine paintings*
- *bacteria—back door to a cafeteria*
- *benign—what you be after you be eight*
- *bowel—letters like a, e, i, o, u*
- *caesarian section—a district in Rome*
- *cardiology—advanced study of poker playing*

- *cat scan—searching for lost kitty*
- *chronic—neck of a crow*
- *coma—punctuation mark*
- *cyst—short form of sister*
- *diagnosis—person with slanted nose*
- *dilate—the late British Princess Diana*
- *dislocation—in this place*
- *enema—not a friend*
- *false labour—pretending to work*
- *genes—blue denim*
- *impotent—distinguished/well-known*
- *labour pain—hurt at work*
- *lactose—people without feet*
- *lymph—walk unsteadily*
- *microbes—small dressing gown*
- *obesity—City of Obe*
- *pacemaker—winner of Nobel Peace Prize*
- *pulse—grain*
- *pus—small cat*
- *secretion—hiding anything*
- *tablet—small table*
- *tumour—extra pair/you die*
- *ultrasound—radical noise*
- *urine—opposite of 'you're out'*

Irony, Satire and Witty Terminology

- *varicose—very close*
- *vein—at what time?*

Then you also have witty definitions which are often chauvinistic:

There is only one perfect child in the world, and every mother has it. There is only one perfect wife in the world, and every neighbour has it.

> *Prospective husband: 'Do you have a book called* Man, the Master of Women*?'*
> *Salesgirl: 'The fiction department is on the other side, Sir.'*

Girlfriends are like chocolates, taste good anytime.
Lovers are like pizzas, hot and spicy, eaten frequently.
Husbands are like dal rice, eaten when there is no choice.

And a few rules of life:

- Lorenz's Law of Mechanical Repair: *After your hands become coated with grease, your nose will begin to itch.*

- **Anthony's Law of the Workshop:** *Any tool, when dropped, will roll to the least accessible corner.*
- **Kovac's Conundrum:** *When you dial a wrong number, you never get an engaged one.*
- **Cannon's Karmic Law:** *If you tell the boss you were late for work because you had a flat tyre, the next morning you will have a flat tyre.*
- **O'Brien's Variation Law:** *If you change queues, the one you have left will start to move faster than the one you are in now.*

14

Outraged Correspondence

Apart from the abusive letter I received calling me 'bastard' when I strongly condemned Jarnail Singh Bhindranwale for spreading hatred, which I referred to in an earlier chapter, the number of vituperative letters in my mail increases steadily.

(A man—though no gentleman, I presume is of the male gender—sends me one every other day addressing me as 'Dear Bum'.) After telling me what they think of my politics, they proceed to make uncharitable comments on my age and lechery. No doubt I invite most of this by what I write. I am cheered to see that greater men than poor I indulged in the same kind of self-exposure and received the same kind of abusive response.

There was the poet, Momin (d. 1851) who put my thoughts in delectable verse over a century ago:

> *There was a young man who was famed among the lovers,*
> *and was for his deeds renowned.*
> *His name was Momin, faith idolatry, the worship of idols*
> *being his sole concern.*
> *No thought he gave to world of religion,*
> *But cared for lovely ladies' charm alone.*
> *He spent his time in leisure, love and joy,*
> *Lost in life's pleasures night and day;*
> *Forever happy, gay and drunk on hope,*
> *Forever smiling like an open bud;*
> *Green like the flask of wine laughing when the sparkling*
> *liquid is poured into the cup.*

Then there was the Lucknowi, Nasikh, who wanted his fleshy desire to be inscribed on his epitaph:

I am a lover of breasts like pomegranates;
Plant then no other trees on my grave but these.

The Urdu poets were certainly more imaginative than I. To wit Atish:

Whenever a bubble by another bubble rose, I thought of her brassiere of finest gauze.

Now I await another crop of outraged correspondence. Don't let me down.

15

Torture by Telephone

*I*f you are always at the receiving end, it can be hell. I can recommend three antidotes to the victims. Do not have your name listed in the telephone directory. Instal a plug by which you can disconnect the instrument till such time as you want to inflict yourself on someone. And as soon as our friends and acquaintances get to know your number, change it.

Caution: Make sure the new number allotted to you did not belong to a doctor, or a lawyer, or a household full of teenage telephone addicts or retired people who have nothing to do besides reading papers, listening to Vividh Bharati and awaiting calls from their 'near and dear ones'. Let me illustrate this from personal experience.

I had changed my telephone number. For some

inexplicable reason, my new number was the old number of an elderly Parsi couple. So six of the seven calls I took went somewhat as follows:

'Hormazd?'

'No.'

'Bearer, Seth *kah gayach?*'

Bearer indeed! I break into my haw-haw Oxbridge. 'I am afraid this is not Mr Hormazd's number any more. I do not know how he is, nor his new telephone number. Please ring "Enquiries".'

A week later, apparently, word must have gone around that Hormazd was ill. No sooner would I plug in the instrument than calls would start pouring in. I avoided plugging till after midnight, when I was sure Hormazd and his friends were fast asleep.

The telephone rang. I switched on the bed lamp. It was 3 a.m. My temper was high. My thinking capacity was very low. The Devil got inside me. A lady's voice demanded to know the health of Mr Hormazd. In my best Parsi Gujarati, I replied, '*Arre, soon kehoon mai. Evan to rate gujri gaya*—he died last night.'

'*O Khodai! Soon kaoch Bawa!*' came the wail.

'*Soon thayyun?*—what happened?'

'*Kon jane—kai poochhoj na*—please...'

I put down the receiver.

Torture by Telephone

I realized too late I had brought trouble on my head. Thereafter the telephone rang again and again. The frantic queries were all the same.

'*Hormazd ne soon thai gayyun*—we are coming over right away...'

'*Mrs Hormazdji ne bolawani* please—call Mrs Homi.'

I grew tired of replying. '*Hormazd ne Dungarwadi lai gaya chhe*—Mrs Homi is heartbroken. She cannot speak.'

But the calls continued. Whenever I plugged the phone in—it rang.

On the third day, I decided to put an end to the nuisance by yelling into the receiver, 'Hormazd, whoever the ass is, is not dead and I couldn't care less whether he dies or lives. But, for God's sake, leave me alone!'

I plugged the phone in and waited. It rang. I picked up the receiver, but before I could begin, an irate old lady's voice came through with searing abuse:

'*Marere mua—Luchcha, Laffanga*, you've been spreading the news that my poor Homi is dead. *Mare taro baap, taro baap no baap tara badha* dear ones! I shall report you to the police. I shall have you arrested...'

16

Pakistani Humour

I did not find any special Pakistani flavour in the jokes about their leaders. One often related about General Ayub Khan I had heard about Indira Gandhi.

The general arrives in Allah's court where there is a large assemblage of the world's great personages. The Almighty honours them by getting up from his throne to shake hands with them. But when General Ayub Khan steps forward to greet his Maker, Allah remains firmly seated on his throne. Later, the angels gather round Allah and ask him about his strange behaviour in discriminating against the distinguished Pakistani.

Allah replies, 'With the others I felt quite safe, but I know that if I left my throne to shake hands with Ayub Khan he would immediately push me away and grab it.'

I heard several jokes about Zia-ul-Haq:

President General Zia-ul-Haq desired to issue a postage stamp to commemorate his two-year rule in Pakistan. The best artist of the country was ordered to draw his portrait: Sam-Browne belt, medals, epaulettes, the works. Millions of stamps were printed and released with great fanfare. After a couple of weeks the president wanted to know how the stamp was doing. He sent for the postmaster general and asked him about the sales.

'General President Sir, I deeply regret to inform you that the stamp is not selling well.'

'Why?'

'Because they do not stick.'

'Why? Have the gum supplier arrested immediately. I will have him flogged publicly.'

'No Sir, there is nothing wrong with the gum,' protested the P.M.G, 'the stamps won't stick because the people spit on the wrong side.'

On Humour

General Zia-ul-Haq while on a visit to India decides to ring up the late Mr Bhutto to find out how he is getting on wherever he is.

He puts in a long distance call. Indian telephones, which have great difficulty in putting through local calls, have no trouble whatsoever connecting him with the nether regions. So General Zia has a brief three-minute chat with Bhutto who assures him he is better looked after than he was in Rawalpindi gaol. General Zia's telephone bill for this long distance call is ₹1,000. This is understandable as hell is a long way away from India.

General Zia returns to Pakistan and decides to have another powwow with the late Mr Bhutto. Pakistan telephones have learnt the ropes from their Indian counterparts and immediately get Mr Bhutto on the line.

General Zia talks to Bhutto for over an hour. He then asks for the bill. It is only ₹15. The general is most impressed but asks his telephone department to explain how a three-minute call from India cost him a thousand rupees while an hour's chat from Pakistan cost only fifteen. Promptly comes the reply, 'Sir, in Pakistan a call to hell is charged at local rates.'

No sooner was General Zia-ul-Haq buried than a whole lot of anti-Zia jokes which were whispered around began to be told openly.

Question: How did they recognize General Zia's body from the debris of the air crash?
Answer: It was the only one firmly clutching the chair it was seated on.

The other one is more macabre in its black humour.

Since all victims of the crash were mutilated beyond recognition, the workers putting bodies in coffins did the best they could, giving each a head, torso, arms and legs, without bothering what belonged to whom. The bodies were solemnly interred in different graves.

The general was summoned by God and reprimanded for the wrongs he had done to the people. 'You will receive a hundred lashes on your buttocks,' was the Divine sentence.

The general was duly tied to a post, his bottom exposed and the jailer began to apply the whip. With each stroke, the general roared with laughter. The Almighty was very surprised at his behaviour and asked, 'Why are you laughing while being beaten?'

'Because the buttocks receiving the lash belong to the American ambassador.'

President Zia-ul-Haq's trusted barber seemed to have become infected by the popular demand for the restoration of democracy.

One morning while clipping the president's hair he asked, 'Gareeb purwar! When are you going to have elections in Pakistan?'

The president ignored the question with the contempt it deserved from a military dictator. At the next hair-cutting session, the barber asked, 'Aali jah! Isn't it time you redeemed your promise to have elections?'

The president controlled his temper and remained silent.

On the third hair-clipping session the barber again blurted out, 'Banda Nawaz, the awam (common people) are clamouring for elections, when will you order them?'

The president could not contain himself anymore and exploded, 'Gaddar (traitor)! I will have you taught a lesson you will never forget,' and ordered his minions to take away the barber and give him ten lashes on his buttocks.

The barber fell at the great man's feet and whined, 'Zill-i-Ilahi (shadow of God) I eat your salt; how can I become a gaddar? I only mentioned elections to make my job easier.'

'What do you mean?' demanded Zia-ul-Haq.

'Every time I utter the word election, Your Excellency's hair stands on edge and is much easier to clip.'

After the last summit meeting between Rajiv Gandhi and President Zia-ul-Haq, the two met privately for a friendly exchange of views. 'What is your favourite hobby?' Zia-ul-Haq asked Rajiv Gandhi.

'I collect jokes people tell about me,' replied Rajiv. 'And what is your favourite hobby, Mr President?'

'I collect people who make jokes about me,' replied Zia-ul-Haq.

Recent visitors to our militant neighbour have brought back a crop of anecdotes bearing on its state of affairs. The first one compares it to its neighbour on the other side, Iran.

Ayatollah Khomeini called on Allah and complained, 'Just and merciful Allah! I have introduced the Islamic code in my country but there has been no improvement in the condition of the people. When will things change for the better?'

Allah thought over the problem for a minute and replied, 'Not in your lifetime.'

Khomeini burst into tears and departed.

The next caller was General Zia-ul-Haq. 'Almighty God, I have also introduced the Islamic code in my country and there has been no improvement in the condition of the people. When will things get better in Pakistan?'

Allah pondered over the problem for a minute and burst into tears and replied, 'Not in my lifetime.'

☺

And two related to the army and military rule:

A peasant travelling by bus from Rawalpindi to Islamabad addressed the man sitting next to him, 'Sir, are you in the army?'
'No.'
'Is your brother or any other relation in the army?'
'No.'
'Is there anyone from your village in the army?'
'No.'
'In that case, you son of a bitch, why the hell have you put your foot on mine?'

☺

Three civilians were hauled up before a military court for assaulting an army captain. When asked to explain, the first accused replied, 'Sir, this man winked at my sister and I felt I had to beat him up to redeem her honour.'

The second accused replied, 'Sir, every girl in the village is like a sister to me. So when this fellow winked at my friend's *sister I joined him in redeeming the girl's honour.'*

The third accused, who was not from the village, replied, 'Sir, when I saw these two men assault the man in uniform, I thought that military rule was over in Pakistan, so I said to myself, why not I also do something for my country?'

Indians enjoy telling jokes about Pakistan. Here are some I have heard.

A gentleman travelled all the way from Islamabad to Karachi to have an aching tooth taken out. The Karachi dentist said, 'Surely you have dentists in Islamabad! You did not have to come all the way to have your tooth attended to.'

'We have no choice. In Islamabad, we are not allowed to open our mouths,' replied the man with the aching tooth.

An issue of *Private Eye* of London has an interesting item in its column 'Funny Old World', about English words banned from usage in Pakistan. It reads:

'The Telecommunications Act of 1996 is perfectly clear,'

On Humour

Muhammad Talib Doger of the Pakistan Telecommunication Authority told a press conference in Islamabad, 'in prohibiting the transmission of messages that are indecent or obscene. We now have the technology to enforce this, so from 21 November, all mobile phone operators are required to screen all text messages, and filter out any words on our list of banned terms. So far, this list contains 1695 words, and more will be added as they come to our attention.'

The move has caused outrage among mobile phone users, with many threatening to challenge the order in court. 'The list is absurd,' said spokesman Shahzad Ahmed, 'it includes phrases like "monkey crotch", flatulence, athlete's foot, kiss ass, fairy, quickie, damn, and "go to hell", even "deeper and harder"'. We are witnessing a ruthless wave of moral policing by the PTA. By forcing telecom operators to filter out these allegedly offensive words to make our society moral and clean, the PTA has made a mockery not only of itself, but of the entire country. Twitter users were both bemused and amused. 'What is an "ass puppy?"' asked one, while another wanted to know 'the vile significance of Yellowman'. Sabina tweeted, 'I think PTA just enhanced the vocab for us. Never knew words like these ever existed.'

Pakistani Humour

A joke that recently did the rounds of Delhi's diplomatic cocktail circuit, though slightly over the line of propriety, deserves to be told because it illustrates the kind of feelings that obtain between Indians and Pakistanis.

The president of the Soviet Union was celebrating his silver jubilee. As head of state he desired that all countries accredited to it should present him with the best of their products. First came the American ambassador with a brand-new Cadillac. The president graciously accepted the gift. It was followed by the British ambassador presenting the latest model of a Rolls-Royce. The president was delighted and desired that his thanks be conveyed to Queen Elizabeth II. The next was the ambassador of Israel. He had brought a new variety of elongated lemon developed in his country. The president was furious and ordered the lemon to be put up the Israelis posterior. Then came the Indian ambassador. He presented a luscious Alphonso mango. The president was not amused and ordered the fruit to be stuffed up the Indian's behind. Having been subjected to this painful insult the Israeli and the Indian ambassadors met in the lobby of Kremlin Palace. The Israeli looked woebegone. The Indian was wreathed in smiles.

The Israeli asked the Indian, 'How can you manage to look so happy after what has been done to you?'

The Indian ambassador replied, 'You've no idea what is

in store for the ambassador of Pakistan. He has brought the largest watermelon developed in his country.'

Yahya Khan, the former Pakistan president, trying to persuade a yokel to volunteer for the Pakistani Air Force, took him inside the aircraft and explained, 'You press this yellow button and the engine will start. Then you press the red one and the plane will fly. It is all very simple.'

'But how do I bring it down?' asked the yokel, puzzled.

'You don't have to bother about that,' explained Yahya Khan. 'Leave that to the Indian Air Force.'

17

Cricketing Humour

Have you noticed that there are hardly any jokes about cricket? I checked up a dozen anthologies of humour and found innumerable stories on golf, baseball, chess, card games—not one on cricket. It's a humourless game. Cricketers take themselves too seriously. But here are a few jokes I found:

Sharmila Tagore rings up the Wankhede Stadium and asks for her husband. 'Madam, the Nawab Sahib has just gone in to bat,' says the voice at the other end. 'Can I take a message or will you ring up later?'

'I'll hang on,' replies the film star Begum Pataudi, 'he never takes very long at the wicket.'

On Humour

The following original story is in untranslatable Punjabi and far too obscene. Try and work it out. It was narrated to me by none other than Bishen Singh Bedi.

Bishen Singh Bedi stands in the centre of a marketplace tossing a cricket ball and addressing passers-by: 'Behno aur bhaiyo!' Soon a large crowd collects round him. Bedi continues to toss the cricket ball and yell: 'Brothers and sisters!'

A man approaches him and asks, 'Sardarji, why don't you say something? See the enormous crowd you have collected.'

Replies Bedi, 'Sir, you have no doubt seen lots of fools play with different kinds of balls on different kinds of playing fields. But I bet you haven't seen so many fools gather around one cricket ball.'

Pakistani cricketers, who do not know the English language well, prepare the answers before a match takes place. After a match was over, Tony Greig interviewed Inzamam-ul-Haq.

Tony Greig: 'So, Inzy, that is fantastic. Your wife is pregnant for the second time.'

Inzamam: 'Mashallah, all the credit goes to the boys. Everyone worked hard for it, specially Afridi. His performance was really fantastic. Also, a good crowd had gathered to see his work.'

18

Being Tipsy

My fondness for drink is legendary. A contributor did an amusing piece about me. It goes like this:

A search party of US soldiers and Indian army men went out on a manhunt to nab Osama bin Laden in his cave in the mountains of Afghanistan. After scouring through numerous caves they came to a large bottle-shaped cavern which had an ominous lamp burning at one end. The search party geared up to capture their prey. Rifles were cocked, machine guns straddled to shoulders and torches beamed out light. 'There he is!' roared out a dozen voices even as they spotted a lone figure seated at a table, who was in the act of raising a half-finished bottle of vodka to his mouth. As the searchers came close to the man, an Indian soldier in their midst exclaimed with appalling loudness, 'Holy cow!'

'What's the matter?' said his companions.

'I know that man—it is not Osama bin Laden!'

'Then who is it?'

'It's...it's...it's Khushwant Singh!' said the Indian soldier, even as he passed out with shock.

'What the hell are you doing here?' asked an American soldier.

'I've been here ever since the Russians left,' said the man, 'the caves are full of it. Free vodka!'

Mir Taqi Mir shared this weakness. I have rendered his popular composition on drunkenness—'*Yaaro Mujhey Maaf Karo, Mein Nashey Mein Hoon*':

Friends forgive me! You can see I am somewhat drunk.
If you must, an empty cup let it be,
For I am somewhat drunk.
As the flask goes round, give me just a sip—
Not full to the top, just enough to wet my lip;
For I am somewhat drunk.
If I use rude words, it is all due to drink
You too may call me names and whatever else you think,
For I am somewhat drunk.

Being Tipsy

Either hold me in turn as you hold a cup of wine
Or a little way come with me, let your company be mine,
For I am somewhat drunk.
What can I do, if I try to walk I stumble,
Be not cross with me, please do not grumble;
For I am somewhat drunk.
The Friday prayer is always there, it will not run away
It will come along with you if for a while you'll stay
For I am somewhat drunk.
Meer can be as touchy as hell when it is his whim
He is made of fragile glass, take no liberty with him;
For he is drunk.'

And a limerick contributed on this subject is as follows:

The old man took martini ten pegs a day without fail
All his friends' entreaties were of no avail.
When he was in some sense
They urged him to try abstinence
He refused, saying it was too late to try a new cocktail!

19

Black Humour

Some people like taking their walks in the open country; others like to stroll through well-laid parks or the seafront. My favourite promenade has always been the cemetery. I have discovered many beautiful ones in different parts of the country where the peace and quiet that reigns can only be described as not-of-this-world. And what a wealth of family history and sentiment engraved on tombstones! There is one at Agra which is older than the Taj Mahal where the remains of many famous European adventurers lie entombed in Mughal splendour with names and epitaphs inscribed in Persian. To people who share this interest, I can recommend many in Calcutta, Madras, Kanpur, Bombay and Delhi.

Our hill resorts have some of the most beautiful graveyards tucked away amidst glades of pine and fir. When I take my annual Himalayan holiday in the autumn I make it a point to revisit these sylvan haunts. I know who rests where; I know when and why he or she died. In every cemetery, there is some tomb which for some inscrutable reason draws more attention to itself than the others. There is one at the bottom of the hill at Kasauli. The tombstone beckons the visitor to take notice. The epitaph reads:

> *Halt stranger!*
> *Do not pass by*
> *As you are now so once was I*
> *As I am now so you will be*
> *Prepare then to follow me.*

Not very great poetry, but sound common sense and so very arresting! I have a posthumous riposte ready on my lips:

> *Reader, pass on!*
> *Don't waste your time*
> *On bad biography and bitter rhyme*
> *For what I am, this cumbrous clay insures,*
> *For what I was, is no affair of yours!*

* * *

Most upper- and middle-class Indian families celebrate birthdays. We were lower-middle class and in my time parents did not even bother to record dates of birth and, therefore, were never able to have horoscopes cast. So some like me chose a suitable date to have a party and receive presents.

With the passage of years, birthdays ceased to be occasions for celebration. Now when I run into one of my peer group we usually exchange information on each other's health. It goes somewhat as follows:

'I see you wear glasses; what strength are the lenses?' (Meaning: Are you going blind?)

'Do you have a hearing problem? Do you use a hearing aid?' (Meaning: Are you going deaf?)

'How many teeth have you left in your mouth?' (Meaning: Do you wear dentures?)

'Do you have to get up at night to urinate?' (Meaning: Do you have an enlarged prostrate?)

Then there are similar queries about blood pressure, diabetes, heart etc.—all related to the question of how much longer have we to go.

These melancholy thoughts come to my mind as I go in for cataract surgery. A few weeks back, I had a few sessions with my dentist. I do my best to avoid my dentist as he is forever finding fault with my teeth and warning me against chewing too much paan. Then one of my lower teeth began

Black Humour

to hurt badly and I had to subsist on a liquid diet for two days. On the first session the dentist took an X-ray of the affected tooth. At the next session he showed me that the rot had spread and he yanked out two of them. Of the original 32, I have only 26 left. I am still a lot better than most people of my age. We don't await our birthdays to remind us of our age—bills of doctors, dentists and opticians keep us informed.

* * *

You have to be old to know what the real problems of ageing are. As an old English proverb goes: 'Only the toad beneath the harrow knows where each point of the harrow goes.'

I am not talking of physical or mental infirmities which come with the years and need special medical treatment. Nor of the indifference of sons, daughters and grandchildren who find their grandparents' growing senility and anecdotage a nuisance and would like them to depart from the world to make life easier for them.

I am not even talking of the shortage of old people's homes where the aged could spend their last days in reasonable comfort and die in peace. What I am talking about is the callous indifference and lack of consideration of the common people towards those who can no longer keep pace with them. Let me give you a few examples from personal life.

For as long as I can remember we have been spending at least one evening of the week with our friend of over 60 years, Prem Kirpal. He lives less than 50 yards from us across the road. Till five years ago we used to simply walk over taking the road divider in our strides. Then the divider became a hurdle—stepping on it became as hard a feat as scaling the Everest; stepping down from it on the other side became even more hazardous. We circumvented the hurdle and found a break in the road divider. The next problem was to wait for a suitable gap in the speeding traffic to get to the middle of the road and wait for a similar break in the stream of cars, buses and scooters coming from the other direction and hobble across as fast as our legs could carry us. Now, Prem Kirpal sends us his car to take us across the 50-yard divide. I am reminded of the Urdu couplet:

Javaani jaatee rahee
Aur hamein pataa bhee na laga;
Isee ko dhoond rahey hain
Kamar jhukaae hooey

(Youth faded away
And we did not as much as
notice it going.)

Black Humour

We are up against another problem, more serious than dining with a friend. In the summer months we go to Kasauli two or three times. I used to drive all the way. Then the traffic on the Grand Trunk Road and the 22 miles from Kalka to Kasauli became too heavy for comfort.

We took to going by train—the Himalayan Queen—to Chandigarh, then by car to Kasauli. Then we had to give up the Himalayan Queen for the simple reason that this train left from and came to different platforms of New Delhi Railway station which entailed going up and down steps of overbridges.

We could not negotiate coming down because of the danger of being knocked down by people running down in a hurry. Now, even though as an ex-MP we could travel free, we go by the Shatabdi Express and pay ₹1,300 each way for the simple reason that the train leaves and arrives on platform number one and there are no overbridges to cross. Even so, boarding and getting off trains has become a nightmarish experience. Stations and platforms are crowded. Everyone seems to be in a desperate hurry to get in or get off the train. The *dhakkam dhakka* (shoving and pushing) can knock down old people and fracture their brittle bones. Travelling by air is only marginally easier. I have to request the staff or some able-bodied fellow-passengers to help me with hand baggage. I realize my days of travel are fast coming to a close.

What are old people to do? *Vaanprastha*—retirement to the jungles—is the prescription suggested by our sacred texts. I am beginning to come to the conclusion that they had the right answer.

* * *

It is commonly held that one should not speak ill of the dead and, of course, joking about them is considered in bad taste. But there is a genre of humour specially devoted to this—black humour. So, finally, some black humour I have written on the subject of death.

I wrote to Badey Mian, whose records decide our destinies, to send for me as I was tired of living. He consulted his registers and replied, 'At the moment all the cells in hell are occupied and there is no room available for you. As soon as a vacancy occurs, I will send for you. Till then hang on and go on with whatever you are doing.'

I was disappointed, as I am tired of living. However, since there is nothing I can do against His wishes, I hang on.

One day in Calcutta, I was waiting for a taxi when a man

about 90 years old looked at my suitcase and asked, 'Where are you going?'

'On a short trip,' I replied.

The old man said, 'I'll be going on a long trip soon.'

Touched, I said, 'Well, we all have to take that long trip one day. If I'm fortunate and live to be your age, I'll be very happy about it.'

His look changed from that of attentive listening to one of impatience. 'Young man,' he retorted, 'I'm going to my grandson in London!'

I have written on the subject of death more than once and have received more letters than I have on any other topic I have written about. So permit me to write one last piece on it.

We have to be constantly reminded that it is not only other people who die. However much we try to put death out of our minds, other people's deaths will remind us of its inevitability.

Of all the gods of the pantheon, the one we cannot appease by prayer, bribery or flattery is Yama. Aeschylus wrote:

Alone of gods death has no love for gifts
Libations help you not sacrifice

> *He has no altar, and he hears no hymns*
> *From him alone persuasion stands apart.*

Unless you commit suicide or are hanged, you will not know when death will come to you.

The prayer in the Psalms, 'Lord let me know mine end, and the number of my days that I be certified how long I have to live,' remains unheard. The older we grow, the more we realize that our end is nearing. To wit Kingsley Amis:

> *Death has got something to be said for it*
> *There's no need to get out of bed for it*
> *Wherever you may be*
> *They bring it to you, free.*

One way to overcome fear of death is to make fun of it. On his 75th birthday, Winston Churchill was asked what he thought about it. 'I am ready to meet my maker. Whether my maker is prepared for the ordeal of meeting me is another matter,' he replied. Lord Palmerston on his deathbed told his physician, 'Die, my dear doctor? That is the last thing I shall do.'

* * *

I haven't come across any really witty epitaphs except in books of nonsensical verse. And I often wonder why we Indians have never indulged in epitaph-composing as a literary form! I have never come across one on a Muslim grave and all the graffiti inscribed at entrances of Hindu-Sikh crematoria are invariably tearful or taken from religious texts. I agree death is no laughing matter but surely what is inevitable need not necessarily be taken with such morbid grimness!

I asked readers to try their hand at writing their own epitaph. The following responses were received:

- Doctor: *The final treatment*
- Author: *Returned with compliments*
- Grammarian: *Correctly spelled out*
- Bishop: *Prayer answered*
- Judge: *The final judgement*
- Horticulturist: *Pruned*
- Merchant: *The single entry*
- Khushwant Singh: *A weekly habit beerfully soiled*
- Psychologist: *Errors corrected*
- Dentist: *Here lies a dentist filling his last cavity*

* * *

My scooter and I, under this stone are stowed. For we watched the gals and not the road!

Epitaph: Khushwant Singh

Here lies one who spared neither man or God
Waste not your tears on him, he was a sod
Writing nasty things he regarded as great fun
Thank the Lord he is dead, this son of a gun.

Acknowledgements

Many of the essays that appear in this volume are versions of pieces that first appeared in *New Delhi, The Tribune, Sunday, Hindustan Times, Illustrated Weekly of India,* and *The Telegraph,* to name a few of the publications that Khushwant Singh contributed to. As the majority of the pieces were taken from typescripts in the possession of the author's estate, it has been difficult to accurately source the name of the publication in which the pieces first appeared. All the essays in the book have been used with permission from the author's estate. Every effort has been made to trace copyright holders and obtain permission to reproduce copyright material included in the book. In the event of any inadvertent omission, the publisher should be informed and formal acknowledgement will be included in all future editions of this book.

Thanks to Vijay Tankha for going through the manuscript and suggesting changes.

Grateful acknowledgement is made to the following who contributed some of the jokes included in this book:

Wazir Chand Didi, Chandigarh; Kotian, Udupi; Vipin Buckshey, New Delhi; R.P. Chaddah, Chandigarh; Reeten Ganguly, Tezpur; B.T. Mody, Bengaluru; K.J.S. Ahluwalia, Amritsar; Ram Niwas Malik, Gurugram; Jai Deb Bajaj, California, USA; Kuldip Salil, New Delhi; Amir C. Tuteja, Washington; Kamal Sharma, Mukerian; J.P. Singh Kaka, Bhopal; Shashank Shekhar, Mumbai; Judson K. Cornelius, Hyderabad; Rakesh Kumar Sharma, Chandigarh; M.L. Batra, Karnal; Rifaquat Ali; Rajeshwari Singh, New Delhi; Raghvir Singh Malik, Rohtak; Niloufer Bilimoria, Mumbai; Priya Nath Mehta, Gurugram; Jayanta Dattagupta, Kolkata; Sriprasad Shukla, Jamnagar; Jagdish N. Varandani, Jaipur; K.R. Thakor, Mumbai.